I dedicate this book to my amazii

given me so much.

MW01073902

Let me tell you a story. This is no normal story; it is a tale of love and loss, of light and dark, of good and evil. It is a story of despair and hope. It is a story of good magic and dark powers. Mostly it is a story about love, and forgiveness. Even the darkest soul can find forgiveness and peace.

A carriage approached the gate. It was the first in what seemed to be a caravan of twenty carriages. Regal and powerful, the carriages were an ominous black, pulled by fearsome black horses. The horses smelled of sulfur, and their sides were lathered with sweat. Their glowing red eyes were terrifying to behold. The driver of the foremost carriage was deathly white, but he looked very strong.

The guards asked, "What are you transporting?"

The driver replied, "Only those things we need to travel comfortably. We are travelers from a distant land. We have come to seek an audience with your king." He said this with a hint of a smile that displayed his overly long canine teeth. The man sitting on the carriage was pleased. The time had finally come. The time for revenge.

He thought back to his time in the wastelands to the north. Nothing but snow and rocks had surrounded them. They had to go to caves to find bats and other things to feed on. He remembered the bitter cold nights. All those decades spent becoming weaker.

There, he and his people had been trapped by powerful magic. Recently he had broken the spell that had bound them. After a full year of planning, now the next hour would help determine success or failure.

The first guard whistled, and a brown haired boy came running over. "Joshua, kindly conduct these carriages to the palace, then guide their leader to the king's audience chamber."

"Yessir!" Joshua replied. Joshua felt uneasy as he escorted the strangers toward the palace. He resolved to find Salen after he had introduced these strangers at the palace.

They left the carriages in the courtyard, and Joshua escorted the strangely white man up to the audience chamber of the king. The man told the guards to announce him as Lord Erip Mav. After they announced him, Joshua slipped out of the room.

The king sat on his throne at the end of the hall. There were five pillars of red agate on each side of the chamber. Between each set of pillars was a statue of a man or a woman. Previous kings and queens of the era, equally spaced and beautifully sculpted. The statues were carved from the most beautiful marble or agate, with a lone jade statue. They held a certain majesty about them, seeming to come alive as one walked through the hall. The first statue on the left was the only one with an inscription. The inscription read, "This is the likeness of Pathorian the Wise, the savior who helped bind the vampires." Erip Mav had to hide his contempt. He hated what Pathorian had done to his people.

Then there was the king, two hundred fifty years old, with a short white beard and shoulder length white hair. The King stood and walked to the center of the room. He pulled out a wand, waved it, and a table appeared. The table had wine and an assortment of breads and cheeses. The king invited Lord Mav forward and inquired, "May I call you Erip?"

Lord Mav replied, "You may, of course, Your Majesty." Erip Mav relished the taste of the bread. It reminded him of certain animals. The wine both tasted and smelled extra fruity. The cheese was also very pungent. Erip Mav avoided the cheese. It reminded him of his mother and her recipes. As his mother had died tragically centuries ago, this saddened Erip.

The king said, "Very well Erip. Erip, you have a very interesting name. May I ask why you were named such?"

Erip replied, "It is a title really. I am one of the oldest and wisest among my people." The king was intrigued.

The king said, "Well, Erip, to what do I owe the pleasure of your visit?" Lord Mav paused for a moment. He looked as if he were in great pain, or concentrating greatly on something. Suddenly he convulsed. The king inquired, "Erip, are you well?"

Erip responded with a strange cry. Like that of a beast, long, high, and shrill. The king yelled for his guards, drawing his sword and his wand. It was then that Lord Mav transformed. As the king's guards stormed into the hall, Erip threw off his cloak and sprouted a very large pair of bat-like wings.

"A vampire!" exclaimed the king. Erip Mav extended a hand out to either side and red lightning jumped from his hands, engulfing the king's guards. They all collapsed where they stood, dead before they hit the floor.

Lord Mav advanced on the king. The king raised his wand and spoke several words in the language of magic, forming a wall of ice around himself. Lord Erip Mav teleported next to the king, grabbing the king's sword. The king ripped his sword away and teleported across the room. Lord Erip Mav produced a wand and a curved sword from the very air. The spells of their duel cracked the floor and knocked over the throne. Three of the statues shattered. Lord Erip Mav twirled his wand and the king froze. Erip strode toward the king. He stood next to the king and hissed in his ear, "The age of weak men like you and your subjects is over. You will all be slaves to the vampires." Lord Erip Mav produced a dagger of bone from his robes and plunged it into the king's chest. Using his other hand, he crushed the king's wand to a powder like a dry leaf. He took the king's crown and placed it onto his own head.

As the king slowly died, light left the palace. Great dark mists began appearing all over the countryside. The palace itself turned black as night, with an eerie red light about it. It was time for the vampires to rule.

. . .

Joshua ran all the way to Salen's mansion on the outskirts of town. He banged on the door. Joshua heard a thud, then a head poked out of a window above him.

"What do you want, boy?" shouted an irritable looking, grizzled man.

"Pardon me, Salen, but I believe that the king may be in danger."

Salen lept from the window, flipping once and landing on his feet. "We haven't a moment to lose. We must hurry if we are to save the kingdom of Orcalias."

Joshua said, "What of the king?"

Salen pointed to the palace. It was engulfed in darkness with an eerie red light about it. Salen said, "The king is dead. We must find his son and act quickly."

"Salen, I believe I know where they are. Didn't the king's family go on a hunting expedition to their cabin? Only the king remained behind, as I recall," said Joshua.

Salen paused and looked to the west; then he turned to Joshua. "My boy, you are my most trusted and strongest apprentice. I have a plan. I will need you to be brave and do exactly as I say. Can you do that?" Salen said.

Joshua quivered; he had never seen Salen this serious before. He was nervous, but he knew Salen to be a wise master. Joshua said, "Salen, I will do what you ask of me. I know that we can save the kingdom together." Salen smiled, a sweet and tender smile. Tears welled up in Salen's eyes as he beheld his apprentice, for what he knew might very well be the last time. "Then take hold of my hand Joshua. I will have to teleport us to our destination if we are to arrive in time."

…

"Salen, I cannot!" said the king's granddaughter. They were standing in the cabin of the king's son, several dozen leagues from the city. They were deep in the mountains to the east, hidden from all using potent dragon magic. They were surrounded by some of the largest trees in the world. It was a very safe place, but with vampires ravaging the land it would not remain safe for long.

"Salen, how can I send my son, the king's heir, away?" Taylee cried as Salen held her. The loss of her grandfather shook her to her very core. As one of the king's grandchildren it was her responsibility to defend the people. She had sworn binding oaths when she had come of age. If she sent her son away she could not accompany him. She had to stay and fight.

Salen said, "Taylee, sending him over the sea is the best."

Taylee composed herself. She said solemnly, "Salen, if I send him across the sea, then what will become of me?"

Salen looked into her eyes, saying, "I do not know. I am sorry. I do not have the gift of seeing."

Taylee stood, walked to a blank wall, and slammed her hand down on it. Boom! The wall was blasted apart, and behind the wall glittered a purple stone. It was beautiful. It looked like an amethyst, and glowed with an inner light. Inside the stone, barely visible, was what appeared to be a baby dragon.

Salen gasped, "Is that what I think it is?"

Taylee nodded, saying, "The egg."

Joshua wrapped the egg up in a bundle. Salen said, "Joshua, take the baby boy. Here is a map. This will lead you safely to the fairies, elves, and dragons. Hold the boy in your arms and I will transport you to the ocean and put you both on a ship. Then I will return here and fight."

When they arrived at the docks, Salen explained the situation to Robger, the captain of the fastest ship. Robger understood that they would not return, but he and his crew were willing to sacrifice their lives to save the future of their people: the great grandson of the king.)

Chapter One
The Battle at The Castle

Salen returned to the city to find it alight with flames of every color. The smell of death was heavy in the air. The ravens and gore crows flew around in small clouds. The fighting had begun in earnest. There was a powerful smell of sulfur in the air. Salen was weak after so much teleporting, but he managed to make it to his home. He found his son with the lieutenants of the army, making plans to retake the palace. "Maug!" said Salen, then he collapsed in a heap on the threshold of his home.

Salen's dreams were strange. Weaving in and out of his dreams were a silver haired baby and a purple dragon egg. Salen jerked awake. He wondered how long he had been asleep. He knew that it had been unwise to teleport so much, or so far. Saving the king's great grandson was highly important. The king had clearly not told his family the prophecies about the boy, else Taylee would not have hesitated to send him away. As Salen came to this realization he opened his eyes.

Feeling more rested, Salen made his way down the stairs. Maug, his son, was in the entryway conferring with other men of the army. He turned and saw his father. "Father, are you well enough to join us?" asked Maug.

Salen grunted, "I feel tolerably well. Tell me the plan."

Salen studied his entry hall as he listened to his lifelong friends describe their plan to retake the palace. Salen looked to his right and saw the painting he had done of his grandmother many years ago. It was the most accurate painting he had ever done. Even in her old age she had a captivating beauty. He saw the vase his son had made while apprenticing under the finest craftsman of the kingdom. The vase was masterfully and artistically rendered, with the face of a lion imprinted on the front. The lion was roaring his victory for the world to hear. Salen then looked to his left. He saw the image of his late wife. Her short wavy hair, her beautiful smile, and her gorgeous eyes stood out to him. He looked up, and saw the mural his children made. It was beautifully rendered, considering the ages of the artists. There were stick figures and crude drawings, but he loved it all the same. When his boys were young he had levitated them up so that they could draw on the ceiling. This had annoyed his wife but the mural had grown on her over the years. He also remembered taking his children on his knees and telling them tales about satyrs and centaurs and unicorns. He had told them of a far away land called England where great wizards and witches lived. He also told them about the Celts, who worshiped nature and practiced magic. He remembered family dinners and the smell of a roast as it came off the fire. He also remembered, with fondness, Maug's first attempt at cooking. They had not been able to get the burnt smell out of the house for weeks afterward. Not to mention the taste of burnt potatoes. He remembered the smells of the flowers his children grew in the back garden. He thought about all of this, and more, while thinking about the great battle that was about to take place.

He refocused his attention on his son. He had made a realization. He would not be coming back from this battle. As he came to this realization, peace entered his heart. He had saved the king's bloodline and would do all he could to protect his friends. He locked eyes with his son, and in that moment he knew that his son had realized what he had. His son stopped speaking and nodded. Then he turned to the other men.

Maug said, "You all have your assignments. Go, and let us avenge the king." He turned to his father, "Are you certain?" he asked.

Salen nodded "Yes, I am." Maug understood that this would be his father's last battle. He did not feel the same peace as his father did, but he was ready to avenge the king.

The troops were organized into three groups. One group was attacking the front gate and groups two and three the east and west gates. Maug and Salen decided to join separate groups. Salen could teleport people into the palace -- this was the plan that they had discussed at length. Maug and Salen had to choose carefully who would be going with Salen. His companions had to volunteer as this was going to most likely be a suicide mission. Five of their best fighters had volunteered. They were Uthard, Penrod, Joseg,

Mang, and Liam. They would teleport into the palace and attempt to rout the vampires. Their plan was most likely futile but fighting in the palace would hopefully distract from the other parts of the army.

Very few people knew how to access the ancient magic of teleportation. Salen was trained in this magic by a fairy, and he had instructed a few others. Royalty instinctively had this power to teleport; it is not entirely known how they did.

The six men, including Salen, grasped hands. At that moment there was a loud thundering and the ground began to shake. "We must hurry!" shouted Salen. He told them all to focus on the audience chamber. Salen concentrated as hard as he could, and they vanished.

They arrived in the audience chamber of the king. It was so dark they couldn't see anything. They looked out the windows and saw the west wing of the palace covered in a black cloud that blotted out the sun. They pulled out their weapons. Salen touched each weapon, causing them to glow with light. There was a vampire sitting on the king's throne wearing the king's crown. The king lay dead on the floor at his feet. The vampire stood, and spoke.

"Gentlemen, have you come to avenge your pathetic king?" The men were angry but they did not act rashly. They spread out into the shape of a six pointed star. White light began flowing from the men. The vampire growled. He snapped his fingers and five vampires appeared behind the men. Their light began to dim. The vampire spoke again "I am Lord Erip Mav! Who are you to stand against me?"

Salen held up his staff, which had a glowing diamond on its tip. As he spoke, the diamond began to swell in brightness, creating a bubble of protective light around the six men. Salen said, "We are come to avenge our King." With that, Salen shouted a clarion war cry and sent a fireball flying at Lord Erip Mav.

. . .

Maug could see that the battle was not going well. The destruction laid before his eyes was incredible. People were fleeing in every direction. Some of the vampires could transform into fearsome creatures, sowing discord in the ranks of men. There was one vampire, clearly the Lieutenant, who was particularly fierce. He did not distinguish between man or woman, old or young. He did not let any escape his clutches. He left behind a trail of bodies. This Lieutenant locked eyes with Maug, and Maug knew that he had to bring him down. He ordered his archers to target that vampire.

Now, while Maug had never successfully teleported, he did know the theory. He knew that one had to concentrate on where one wanted to go and imagine oneself there. Maug believed that he would have to access teleportation in order to kill this Lieutenant.

Suddenly the Lieutenant screamed. An arrow was protruding from his eye. He pulled it out and threw it with such strength at the man who shot it that it went straight through him. The man was about ten feet from Maug. The vampire teleported next to the man, latched onto his neck, and began to drink his blood, right there on the battlefield. Maug pulled a dagger from his belt and threw it with all his might at the vampire. The vampire flicked his wrist up and caught the dagger. He stared at Maug, his lips ruby red.

"Not while I am here will you feast from the lifeblood of my men!" shouted Maug. Maug pulled out his broad sword and advanced on the Lieutenant. "What is your name?" he demanded.

The Lieutenant considered him for a moment, "I am Cardolo, brother to Lord Erip Mav. It is the age of vampires now, you weak human." He raised his hand and a cloud of bats flew from all directions and converged on Maug. Maug plunged his hands into his cloak and pulled out his wand. He held it up, and a bubble of white energy surrounded him. Whenever a bat struck the bubble, the bat would die. He had created a shield against the darkness. He knew that these were no ordinary bats, and that they would turn him into a vampire if he was bitten. Soon he was surrounded on all sides by a waist high pile of dead bats.

"Is that all you can throw at me, vampire?" said Maug. He was ready. His wand was a wand of purity, for it had the hair of an angel inside. His wand could protect from any darkness, and cure any poison. Any kind of wand was rare, but angel hair wands were among the rarest of all. The vampires were not prepared for it, but they rallied to their Lieutenant.

Maug knew that he would have to kill Cardolo. According to legend, lesser vampires could be killed by decapitation. Higher or older vampires, sometimes known as Elder Vampires, could only die if one drove a silver stake through the vampire's heart. On very rare occasions one had to put a clove of garlic in the vampire's mouth as well. Maug did not know if this was true, and he did not know how to tell the difference between a higher vampire and a lesser vampire. But he was certain that the Lieutenant was a higher vampire. Suddenly Maug realized he was surrounded.

Maug fought as he had never fought before. Vampires did not process pain the same way that humans did. He had to deal them injuries that were difficult to heal before he could decapitate them. Quickly he was surrounded by mangled bodies. He would take time every few minutes to decapitate several injured vampires. He was relieved when their heads did not reattach. This meant that he was only fighting lesser vampires. Yet he was amazed at their strength. If not for his magical power, he would have been overcome.

Maug fought and he fought. He began to weaken, and he began to be afraid. He was afraid that he would not survive. He was not ready to die. So he continued to fell vampires at a prodigious rate. Soon he was joined by one soldier, then two, then a whole battalion had joined him. Archers, swordsmen, spearmen, pikemen, and even a few wand users surrounded him. He took a moment to catch his breath. A healer ran forward and began to heal him of his most grievous injuries. When Maug could walk steadily and wield his weapons, he told the healer to go elsewhere to heal others. The healer reluctantly agreed.

On and on, Maug fought. The minutes stretched into hours. He began to wonder if the battle would ever end. He reached out telepathically to the archers and the men at the ballisti. He told them to attack the Lieutenant with everything that they had. He instructed them to use their phoenix feather arrows to weaken him. They all began to launch their arrows and suddenly the Lieutenant was engulfed in flames.

He looked at Maug and screamed his rage. Suddenly he disappeared, leaving the flames and the arrows behind. Everyone began looking around. Maug was afraid. Suddenly the battlefield was gone.

Maug had never teleported before, but he understood how it was supposed to work. This sensation was exactly what they had described. Suddenly he was standing on the top of a snow covered mountain. He looked to the west. He realized that he was dozens of leagues from the battlefield. He was alone. No one was there to help him.

He turned and saw The Lieutenant looming over him. He was a head taller than Maug; blood dripped from his lips. "Hello Maug," he said. The reek of blood and sulfur clung to the Lieutenant. It assailed Maug in waves. His voice was powerful. So powerful that Maug had a desire to obey that voice. The voice was soft and piercing, almost loving. The Lieutenant said one word. "Bow." Maug sank to his knees.

Maug's mind was roiling with thoughts. Then, suddenly it went blank. Not only did his mind go blank but the reek was gone, instead he smelled his favorite smells. Venison, and freshly baked bread, and dwarven mead. He felt so good obeying that voice. There was only that voice. Maug wanted to hear the voice again. It was like an addiction. He needed to hear the voice, and obey it. Then it spoke again and he felt peace.

"Maug, I need to know where the king's great-grandson is," said the voice. "Maug, please tell me."

Maug opened his mouth to speak. Then many things happened in his mind at once. He realized that this was a trick. He was aware of his pain, but it didn't bother him. Then his pain went away again. He could not reveal the location of the king's great-grandson because he did not even know it himself. The power influence of the lieutenant's voice began to fade. As it did, Maug began to feel pain. The pain was excruciating. But as Maug fought the pain he began to realize where he was and what was happening. He was suddenly filled with horror.

He could not remember if he had divulged anything to the lieutenant. His voice had been so powerful, like drinking truth serum. All of the knights sworn in service to the king had to take truth serum to learn how to fight it. Fighting truth serum wasn't nearly this painful. He screamed from the agony. Then, a voice deep inside him spoke to him. "Maug, you have to fight. Maug, focus. You must fight. You have it within you to teleport. You must use the silver stake." Maug didn't know if it was a vision, or a telepathic communication, or his inner psyche. But he knew it was right. He had to use the silver stake and to teleport.

The lieutenant produced a bright orange whip from his robes that glowed with magic. He began to whip Maug. Over and over the whip came, crack, crack, crack. The voice spoke, "Maug, you must know where the king's great-grandson is. I need you to tell me." With every word his pain ceased, and then when the voice stopped he screamed in agony.

He looked up, into the eyes of the Lieutenant. He wanted more than anything to be behind the Lieutenant. He blinked, and suddenly he was standing behind the Lieutenant. He plunged his hand into his robes and withdrew the silver stake. With all the strength he could muster he plunged the stake into the Lieutenant's back, through his heart and out his chest. The Lieutenant let out a screech that chilled the marrow in Maug's bones. Then the Lieutenant thrashed, and exploded into a cloud of black sand. As the sand fell, Maug knew that his opponent was dead.

He had done it. He had killed the Lieutenant. He was shocked at his success. He suddenly collapsed from all his wounds. He was conscious and in excruciating pain. He wasn't sure if he would be able to teleport back to the castle, but he had to try. For a few minutes he would just lie here, and recover.

. . .

Uthard, Penrod, Joseg, Mang, and Liam turned in unison and converged upon the five vampires behind them at the same moment that the fireball knocked over Lord Erip Mav and sent him flying. Each man was wreathed in a white light of protection. They moved at supernatural speed. But so did the vampires. They began to fight in earnest.

Within a few moments Liam was on the floor bleeding. The vampire who had been fighting Liam began to attack Mang. Mang struck the vampire upside the head, knocking it out, and continued to duel his own vampire. Blow by blow, stroke by stroke, he began to gain the upper hand. They were fighting in earnest. Any blow could have brought death if not for their strength. Mang grabbed the vampire and bodily threw him into a pillar. Then he smote off the vampire's head. The vampire crumbled into black sand.

Uthard was dueling his own vampire. They were ducking and weaving around each other. Blow by blow they both acquired a series of cuts and bumps and bruises everywhere. The ground around them began to crack. Suddenly the vampire waved his hands, and Uthard was wrapped in chains. Uthard broke free, and wrapped the chains around his attacker. Uthard left him there, chained to a pillar. Penrod and Joseg were dueling their vampires as well. After long and perilous fighting their vampires were defeated.

All of this took place within minutes. It felt like hours, but things often do feel this way in battles like this.

Lord Erip Mav stirred. He arose from where he had fallen and snapped his fingers. Uthard, Penrod, Joseg, Mang, and Liam froze. They were unable to move and unable to help in the battle. Salen shouted, a cry of frustration. He knew his moment was near. Erip Mav screamed, an unearthly sound.

Salen knew it was hopeless, but if the kingdom was going to collapse into anarchy he wanted to know why. He wanted to know why the king was dead. He wanted to know why this madness was happening. "Why? Why have you done this terrible deed and killed our king?" Salen cried. "Don't you know that this whole land will now be plunged into darkness? Our crops will not grow properly. Our herds will give birth to one eyed fiends. Lycanthropes will appear in the land. People will be poisoned on the crops they eat. Rivers will turn to blood. Demons may even come back to this land from the netherworlds they were banished to. You have cursed this land. You have opened this land to the dark powers. Why? I demand you tell me!"

Lord Erip Mav wiggled his fingers and chains snaked up and bound Salen in place. Erip laughed, a high, cold, cruel laugh that made the hairs on Salen's neck stand on end. Erip began to speak. His voice had a dreamy and powerful quality, similar to that of other elder vampires. He said "Why would I tell you anything?" Lord Erip Mav then paused. He was considering the wizened old man before him. He decided to toy with him a little. Toying with this man couldn't hurt anything. So Erip decided to share his plan with the doomed man.

Lord Erip Mav spoke, he said "Well, old man. Why don't you first tell me your name? Then I shall entertain whether or not I will tell you."

Salen knew that it was hopeless. He knew that he would not be able to kill this Lord Erip Mav, or whatever his name was. He decided his name would not hurt anything. "My name is Salen." He said. Lord Erip Mav brayed with laughter.

He began to speak again, "Salen? The Salen? The King's best friend? His right hand man? Trainer of the guard? Former Captain of the Guard? That Salen?"

Salen sighed, "Yes, that is me."

Again Lord Erip Mav laughed. "Oh, how the mighty have fallen. Let me tell you why I am doing what I am doing. Humanity has ruled these lands for two millenia. You are a disgusting race. You have neither the purity of the fairies, the wisdom of the elves nor the power of the dragons. You fear what you do not understand. You banished the demons. You banished us. Even the elves and the dragons have withdrawn from you over the long centuries.

"I have slain your king. He was pitiful and pathetic. I will rule this land. I will unleash the demon-kind from the netherworld where your ancestors trapped them. I will be the king. And once I have enslaved all of humanity I will descend upon the dragons, the elves, and the fairies. I will wrest their magic secrets from them, and they will be slaves to my kind. This planet will fall into anarchy, and when it does I will seek the ancient magic of portals and conquer other planets. I will become the ultimate vampire overlord." As he was speaking Lord Erip Mav had returned to the throne. He set it back upright, and sat down. He was wreathed in darkness. Salen knew he could not kill this ancient being. But he was hopeful that he could injure him.

It was at this moment that Lord Erip Mav screamed. It was a different scream, a scream of pain, a wounded scream. "NO!!! Cardolo! How could you die?!" Salen knew his moment had come. He teleported out of the chains and next to Erip Mav. He plunged a silver stake into Erip Mav's back. Erip Mav turned, and as he did so Salen cut off his left arm. Erip Mav screamed in pain, turning around. He pulled the silver stake from his back. Then he plunged the stake into Salen's stomach.

Latching onto Salen's neck, Erip Mav drained Salen in a few moments. Because there had been a silver stake in his body he could not regrow his arm. He was in pain. He lay on the floor.

His third in command appeared in the throne room. "My Lord?" he said.

Lord Erip Mav looked up. "Give the order! I want the leaders of all the cities turned into vampires. I want to OWN THIS LAND!" He screamed the last three words.

Marlova, the third in command, nodded. "It will be done my Lord, even as you have said. Your wish is our command. We are but humble servants." With that Marlova vanished.

With that order the vampires were able to quickly rout the remaining fighters. Turning the leaders into vampires allowed them to enslave the entire kingdom quickly. Because the people were not prepared for the might of the undead, it took the vampires mere hours to do this. Those that escaped fled to the sewers and mountains. The vampires had completely taken over the kingdom. All was lost. Uthard and Penrod, who were the king's grandsons and could teleport, managed to escape. Joseg, Mang, and Liam were not so lucky. They were taken and chained in the dungeon.

Uthard and Penrod went their separate ways. Uthard went to the sewers to help organize the rebellion, and Pendrod went to the mountains to search for Maug.

Chapter Two
Searching for Survivors

The vampires began to search for those who survived their take over. Three months after the takeover, it was estimated that more than half the kingdom was still unaccounted for. This disturbed Lord Erip Mav greatly. He did not know what to do about this. He knew that there would be some people to escape his clutches. He accepted this. When he unleashed demon-kind on the world those who were able to hide would be found. The trouble was with the sheer number who escaped.

His brother was dead and that was a crippling blow to their cause. Cardolo had been a great warrior. He wanted to punish the man who had slain him; unfortunately he didn't know who that man was. He also wanted to extinguish the king's bloodline, or at least to corrupt it. He knew that two of the king's grandsons had escaped. But he did not know much more. Nobody was talking. He was angry.

Erip Mav sat on the former king's throne twirling the crown around his fingers. The crown was remarkable even by human standards. He suspected that it was made by dwarves. Ugh, the thought of dwarves disgusted him. He did not know why. Elves disgusted him too. Dwarves, like elves, could not be turned into vampires. Dwarves did have a dark side, if they could be corrupted with the gold sickness. The gold sickness was a fever of sorts. It could affect any race, but only dwarves and dragons reacted so severely to it. They became jealous and possessive. When corrupted by the gold sickness, they would not release anything that came into their possession.

Then there were the fairies. They were supposedly incorruptible. Unless of course they fell. Their fallen state was a sickly state where they did not have access to certain of their magic powers.

As he sat pondering on his throne, suddenly Erip Mav became aware that someone was speaking to him. "My Lord?" said John. John was a human slave. He had betrayed his friends as soon as the vampires had taken over. He was Erip Mav's token human. Erip Mav almost considered him a pet.

"Yes John?" said Erip Mav. He was angry. Nobody had brought him good news in months. They had been unable to locate the two known missing members of the king's family. It had only been a few days since they had captured the king's granddaughter in the mountains. Her son was not with her. He had ordered her taken to the dungeon. He would torture her later to learn the location of her son.

"My Lord, I crave your pardon," said John. "But I believe that I have good news for you." Erip Mav paused, and stood. Gliding over to John he placed his hand on John's cheek.

"My dear John, if you do not have good news for me I may no longer have a use for you. Tell me what have you found."

John gulped, visibly afraid. "My Lord, I believe that we have located one of the king's grandchildren. Here, in the sewers of the city," said John.

Erip Mav crowed with delight. He had not been this excited since riding into the city the day that he had killed the king. "You have?" he demanded.

John gulped. "Well my Lord, there is someone who has been sabotaging things and setting people free. He always eludes our scouts." John was not the only human slave that they had working for them. But he was the most loyal. If John was right maybe they could finally discover the whereabouts of the king's great grandchild. As loyal as John was, though, Erip Mav knew better than to trust him.

"John, you have done very well. I will not kill you today. We must set traps for this man. We will find him. He will be mine," Erip Mav purred.

He dismissed John with instructions on how to lay some of the traps. He was excited. He felt the draw of the hunt. But he must not allow himself to be distracted. His time would come. Soon enough he would learn what he wanted to know.

Destroying the king's bloodline was vital if the legends were true. According to the legends in the dark parts of the land, the king's bloodline would open up correspondence with the elves. The elves were known to correspond with the dragons. If the dragons returned to this part of the land then all would be lost for the dark creatures like himself.

. . .

Maug gasped. He had woken from a terrible dream. In this dream vampires had attacked the palace. He opened his eyes, realizing he was not at home. He was under a pine tree. Not a dream, he realized. That had really happened. Vampires had really attacked the palace. Then the battle must have happened too. He looked down. His body was whole, his injuries gone. He wondered how long he had been asleep. Judging by how things looked around him it had been quite some time. It seemed to be a different season, but he could not be sure.

He looked around himself, placing his location. He knew this area quite well. It was near the cabin he had helped his father build when he was a young man. They were about a thirty minute walk from the cabin. If he remembered there was also a tree house nearby with survival equipment and — more importantly — weapons. There were also some very powerful talismans there. He did not know all of them. But he knew that they could help him. The Staff of Nolan was among them.

The Staff of Nolan was an ancient talisman of incredible power. Supposedly it was given to Nolan by the Ancient One who helped lock demon-kind in the netherworld. It was an artifact so powerful that even his father had chosen not to use it. With vampires having taken over the land, maybe it was time.

Maug got up and began walking around, adjusting his simple tunic as he did so. A few paces away he found a small fire with a pot of stew. He began to eat ravenously. He had no idea how long it had been since he had eaten. The pot was huge, yet he ate the entire pot of stew. He wished that he had some wine, or even mead with which to wash down the stew. The stew had been amazing. He suddenly felt very tired again. He ambled his way back over to the pine tree, where he lay down and fell asleep.

He was running along the countryside. He was being chased by a powerful vampire. He did not know what to do. The vampire was coming closer. He ran and saw a canyon to his left. He ducked inside the canyon and continued running. The canyon was long, and Maug was tired. He did not know if he could keep going. He pushed on, and kept running. He heard a voice behind him.

"I will catch you, Maug," shouted the voice. Maug did not dare turn around. He was afraid that it would slow him down. He could sense that the vampire was gaining on him.

His fear grew worse. The canyon was a dead end. He was cornered -- there was nowhere to go. Suddenly chains snaked out of the ground and bound him in place. He could not move. The vampire advanced on him. Coming closer and closer, soon the vampire was so close that he could smell the blood on it's breath.

"You are mine now!" it shouted. The vampire plunged its fangs into Maug's neck. Maug screamed, and then he awoke.

. . .

Hiding in the sewer was disgusting business. Uthard knew it was what had to be done. So he waded through the sewers underneath the city, visiting the oldest homes and organizing the people to rebel. He had also been able to conduct a fair amount of sabotage. This part was fun. Either setting explosions at key places throughout the city, or breaking into the lesser dungeons to set people free and help them flee to the countryside. He had organized a fair number of people to rise up and fight from the sewers when the time came. His sons had gone to the five other main cities to recruit and organize. It was not as dangerous as being in the main city.

Uthard did not know anything about his brother Penrod or his sister Taylee. He hoped that his nephew had escaped. He was very concerned. Penrod was supposed to find Maug; he hoped that Penrod had succeeded. Taylee, on the other hand ... he had no idea what had happened to her, or her son. His nephew was a mere babe, and there were prophecies that could refer to the boy. He was uncertain, though; nobody knew to whom the prophecies referred.

Uthard was worried about the rest of his family, his wife and his daughters. He did not know what had happened to them. He had no illusions about their safety: the vampires would probably use them as blood slaves to sate their desire for blood if they were caught. He hoped that they had managed to escape.

Uthard was still somewhat shocked by this whole affair. He thought that all vampires had been destroyed or at least locked away with demon-kind in the netherworld. The vampires had been so powerful. He did not know where their raw power came from. Maybe they had a connection to demon-kind, and their inherent darkness. He did not know.

He was currently traveling to the house of a man named John. This John had contacted him asking for assistance escaping the vampires and it was Uthard's duty to act and help him. The foul sludge in the sewer was absolutely terrible. Unfortunately he was not a strong magician and could not cleanse the air in front of him. As he traveled he thought of potential strategies on how to thwart attempts to capture him.

Uthard checked his surroundings and looked up. He realized that without trying he had ended up where he needed to be. He saw the crudely drawn six pointed star drawn on the door. Uthard and John had agreed that this would be the sign left so that Uthard would know he was at the right place.

He entered the house through the cellar. "John?" He called. Crack! Something smashed into the back of his head. Dazed, he wheeled around to see what had happened. He saw Erip Mav standing over him. He tried to teleport but he could not, something was blocking his way. Erip Mav laughed.

"Dark anti-teleportation magic!" he said. Crack! Another blow to the back of Uthard's head and he was out cold.

. . .

Maug's head was swimming. He felt someone slapping his face. He could hear someone calling his name, but it was as if he heard it from across a large field. Slowly the voice got closer, and closer, and closer. As he smelt the powerful aroma of smelling salts his eyes snapped open. Someone was standing over him but he couldn't recognize them. He tried to raise his hands but he couldn't. Slowly, very slowly the person above him came into focus. He recognized Penrod. He immediately felt relief. Pendrod would be able to help, they would be able to get back to the battle together.

Maug stood up and his head began swimming. He tittered, then he collapsed in a heap. "Maug, you are in no position to do anything!" said Penrod forcefully. He led Maug over to the fire and sat him down. He pressed a cup of chamomile tea into Maug's hand. Maug grew hysterical.

"We have to return to the battle! We have to go! Salen needs our help. He..." Maug stopped and stared at Penrod. "What are you doing here?! You went to fight the head vampire. Wha..." Penrod interrupted Maug.

"Listen to me. Maug, I am sorry, but your father is dead," said Penrod. Maug dropped his cup of tea. Penrod caught it with magic and returned it to his hands.

So Penrod told the tale of what had transpired at the palace. He explained about their fights with the vampires, and their terrible duel. He explained the intimate details of how Salen had died. How Salen had severed the lead vampire's left arm, and how Uthard was rallying resistance in the main city and his sons were spread across the other five major cities. He explained how they had a plan to retake the kingdom. Maug listened intently, and he liked what he heard. What he didn't like was the time frame. Supposedly this plan would take fifteen or more years to put together as they had to recruit dwarves. But Maug knew Penrod to be a wise man. If he thought that they should recruit the dwarves then recruit the dwarves they would.

. . .

Erip sat on his throne. His newly won throne. He savored this emotion. He now also had a plan. He would turn the king's granddaughter Taylee. Instead of wiping out the king's bloodline he would corrupt it. Once bitten, Taylee would become attracted to vampires. Erip would never force her; that was not right. But he was quite irresistible, and once she was a vampire she would absolutely fall for him. Then he would have a son, and he would transfer the stewardship of the kingdom to this rightful heir, while he pursued the release of demon-kind. The plan was pure genius.

There was a knock on the chamber door. One of his henchmen appeared and said, "Here is Taylee as you requested, Master." Erip conjured a table and invited Taylee to join him. As he walked forward she spat on the floor at his feet. He teleported behind her and latched onto her neck, biting her in the way that would transform her. She fell to the ground. He snapped his fingers and the table disappeared. He sat on his throne and waited. The more she fought the change the longer it would take and the more it would hurt her. He enjoyed it when they fought the change — it made them more powerful vampires. He had a suspicion that she would make a very powerful vampire.

It took days for her to transform. Erip was afraid that he had killed her. But eventually she did turn into a vampire. When she awoke she was hungry. It was better for new vampires to feed on living animals. So Erip had some animals brought into the throne room for her to feed on. She was very sickly for a while. Eventually she regained her wits and her senses. She asked to be trained in the arcane arts of black magic. Over the next five years she was trained in the dark arts of black magic. Soon she was almost his equal in magical strength. Eventually there was a spark of romance. She reached out first: she asked him to hunt with her. He agreed. Hunting had never been so exhilarating for him.

He began to court her and they fell in love. Their passion for each other was unequaled. They went on outings to the far reaches of the kingdom. Shortly before their wedding, they locked the rest of the king's family in the dungeon. They turned Uthard into a monkey. They captured Uthard's entire family. They turned them all into various animals and kept them as pets in the dungeon. Soon the day came and they were married.

Their wedding day was a day of darkness. Dark creatures flocked in from all over the kingdom. There were imps, jinn, wendigos, minotaurs, shades, ghosts, fallen angels, arachnaedaes, gorgons, and many others besides. They were showered with gifts and dark talismans. Their power only grew. They seem unstoppable.

With their wedding the entire kingdom collapsed into darkness. The King, Lord Erip Mav, and his new Queen Taylee, Empress of Darkness, ruled over the kingdom. With a member of the royal family ruling at his side nobody could really refute his claim to rule. True, they were vampires, but still the strong were the ones who should rule.

Soon Taylee was with child. The announcement spread throughout all the land. Erip went all over the countryside making sure that his human slaves were doing his bidding. He had statues erected depicting him and his queen. He also had statues erected depicting his lieutenants and one in honor of his brother Cardolo.

Having grown tired of not having two hands Erip traveled to the Ice Caves in the north, and sought Talmarian the Jinn to help him. After weeks of hard negotiating, Talmarian agreed to use powerful dark magic to fashion for him a hand made from a combination of metals that fell to earth from the sky. The hand moved like a human hand, and felt like a human hand except it was a little cooler. It was also indestructible, and different in color.

He returned to his home at the palace to find that his wife was almost ready to give birth. Soon she delivered a healthy vampire boy. Over the next fifteen years Erip relied on his most trusted confidants to handle the affairs of the kingdom while he helped to raise his son.

. . .

When his son was about fifteen years old, Erip received word that Maug and Penrod had been located far away in the mountains to the south. Penrod was the final member of the royal family. And Maug was the son of Salen, the rightful Captain of the Guard. Erip realized that if he captured them he would finally have a grip so tight on the kingdom that none could escape. There were of course the fishermen to the west, but he wouldn't bother himself with them. They were a small and pitiful group, totally unworthy of his attention.

Erip planned and schemed, and finally he was ready. He had come up with a trap to capture Penrod and Maug at last. His spies had informed him that they had opened up a correspondence with the king of the dwarves over the last fifteen years and that they were plotting to overthrow him. This was something that he could not allow. He himself went to the king of the dwarves in disguise. He bound King Blackfoot Irontoe with a curse so powerful he had no choice but to obey him. And with this curse he laid his plan to catch Maug and Penrod.

Chapter Three
Maug's Fate

Erip was getting impatient. His plan to capture the last two key men on his list was about to reach fruition and yet he felt uneasy. He did not like feeling uneasy. After so long plotting and scheming Maug would finally be his. Penrod would also be his, and he thought Penrod would probably make a good slug in his collection of transformed royals. In their transformed state they could not use magic. They also could not assist anyone in overthrowing him. He knew that it was potential foolishness on his part to keep them alive. He did not care. The demons would enjoy torturing them.

Some of his advisors had suggested that they conquer the coast and venture into the land of elves and dragons. Erip disagreed completely. They argued long and hard. Those who believed that they should go conquer the elves argued that they could use dark magic to change the elves into something else and conquer them. Then they should infect the dragons with gold sickness and it would make them easier to control. Then they could use the dragons to open up the portals to the netherworld.

Erip refused to use the dragons. While it was true that potent dragon magic could open up portals to the netherworld where the demons were banished, he preferred to find the ancient dark books to learn how to open and control the portals himself. He had to assert his authority as the eldest vampire to make his underlings agree to his plan. His plan was longer, and it required the game of patience. His men were not as patient as he was. They got angry whenever plans took extra time.

The curse on King Blackfoot Irontoe was still holding strong. Irontoe would obey his every word. Erip put a dark bubble around the palace. When someone teleported into town it would alert him. Then he told Irontoe to move some of his men into the sewer.

Once those men were in the sewer Penrod and Maug would believe that it was safe to enter the city. Once they did, they would be his. His underlings wanted to do things on their own timeline.

They also wanted to exploit his son. He would not allow either path. He was the King and the eldest vampire. His underlings would obey him. He loved his son. Nobody would ever touch his son or use his son while he was alive.

. . .

"Maug. Maug! Wake up!" said Penrod. They were in a cave together. They had been sleeping rough while searching for the were-kind.

"Penrod, what do you want? I am trying to sleep," said Maug. Penrod grew frustrated. Maug had become increasingly short tempered with him. Penrod knew why; Salen, one of the greatest warlocks in over ten thousand years and Maug's father, had been struck down by a vampire.

Penrod left the cave; he needed to give Maug time. There was a wolf pack nearby; perhaps he could go converse with them. Speaking wolfish was fun, but difficult. Humans didn't have the right mouth shape to speak wolfish very well. But he was passable. He had conversed with these wolves. They told him that their leader sought an audience with him. Maug would be fine until he came back.

Penrod began to run. He could run almost as fast as a wolf. It was said that one of his distant ancestors was were-kind but nobody really knew for sure. After what felt like mere moments, but was closer to an hour, he reached the cave where the wolves were staying.

He walked into their camp openly, and with arms outspread. Camp isn't really the right word, but it was the word that he had been raised calling it. Wolves camped with their packs. He looked around, his eyes downcast. To make eye contact without invitation was a threat in their culture. There were thousands of wolf packs scattered across the world. There were several hundred that had sought refuge in their kingdom during the wolf wars.

Suddenly the Alpha stalked out of the cave. He had pure white fur, a testament to his age. He was regal, and he was large. Huge would be a more apt word to describe his size. With paws the size of a human face, eyes as black as night, claws the color of silver, and canines several inches long, he was a sight to behold. He emitted the musky scents of fur and dirt.

He began to bark and grunt; suddenly he sprang forward and tackled Penrod. He opened his jaws, and licked Penrod's face repeatedly. Penrod pushed him off with a smile. Then Penrod stood and spoke. "White-Tail, my old friend, how are you?"

White-Tail drew a message in the dirt; yes, wolves can write. Or at least some of them can. *I am well my friend, but there is a great evil in the land. What are we doing to stop it?*

Penrod sighed. "White-tail, I do not know. Salen is dead. My grandfather, the king, is dead. I do not know what to do. You wolves have a heavenly connection and you are very wise. You are also very brave. What advice do you have?"

White-Tail paused, then began to write. *Penrod, there is a prophecy. The Silver-Haired-Rider is the name of this prophecy. It speaks of many things, and I cannot reveal it to you. You must read it for yourself. There is a copy of the prophecy in Salen's*

treehouse. Maug should know how to access it. Go, and return
when you need our help.

Penrod bowed and thanked the wolves in their own tongue. They howled with laughter at his pronunciations. He was on the way back to the cave where he left Salen when he ran into a dwarf. (It would be more accurate to say that he knocked over the dwarf.)

"Kakan!" exclaimed the dwarf. He was a red bearded dwarf, and his golden mail armour denoted his high status.

"Master dwarf, what can I do for you?" inquired Penrod.

"Ah, master Penrod. I have been sent by my king, His Majesty King Blackfoot Irontoe. He has sent the dwarves into the sewer of the city. We are ready to help you enter the palace. Will you guide me to Maug?" asked the dwarf.

"Yes, let us go to Maug."

They arrived at the cave where Maug was sleeping. Maug was startled but happy to see the dwarf. This meant that they could enter the city. They made their preparations and departed to the dwarven kingdom to confer with Irontoe before they entered the sewers.

It took them almost a full day's journey but they eventually arrived at the dwarves' mountain. They entered the iron doors, not knowing that their lives were about to change dramatically.

The king accepted them into his audience chamber. They bowed before Irontoe, as befitted one of his stature in dwarf society. When Irontoe spoke, his voice was like the shifting of great rocks, very gravely, with deep undertones of hoarse bass. The earthy aroma of dirty rocks pervaded the cavern.

"Gentlemen, I have stationed twelve of my greatest warriors at key points in the sewers. They will obey your command and hopefully help you retake the city. They are also able to bend stone with magic. All dwarves can, but these twelve are among the strongest. Will this please you gentlemen?" Penrod and Maug bowed deeply; it was much more than they had hoped for.

Maug spoke, "Your Majesty, are you alright? Your eyes seem very glassy."

Irontoe smiled. "I am fine, just weary. This darkness in the land is seeping into my domain. I fear nothing can escape it." They once again bowed to the king and he dismissed them.

Maug was very concerned. Once they were out in the open air he spoke to Penrod. "My friend, did Irontoe seem well to you?"

Penrod sighed. "I think we have enough concerns with our own kingdom, without adding the state of our neighbors to our burden." Maug reluctantly agreed. The clasped hands and teleported.

During the teleportation they felt something strange, like a dark pulse. They arrived in the sewers and made their way toward the palace. The city was huge. The palace itself was two square miles. The city was twelve square miles, with the palace in the center. They met up with two dwarves at the entrance to the sewer and began their journey through the filth.

It was filthy, the squelching sound the ground made. The smell was absolutely dreadful. And the rats! The rats were as big as dogs down here in the sewer. The walls were covered in centuries of slime. There were also supposedly sewer monsters. Nobody had ever seen one, though, so they were generally accepted to be a myth.

After walking through the filthy sewer for what felt like days, but was really only about seven hours, they arrived at the palace. They could of course just have teleported into the palace directly, but they had decided to go with this. Their spies told them that Erip Mav had set up warning systems, a magical net, to tell him if anyone teleported into the palace. There were secret passages in the palace, and they could use them to approach the king's chamber and the throne room undetected. They came to the secret door into the palace, and pushed it open.

It was odd, there should have been a dwarf waiting here for them, but the passage was empty. They proceeded with their plan anyway. They had seen the dwarves at the sewer entrance and were not overly concerned. They first went to a washroom to remove the stench so as not to give away their presence with the smell.

Reaching the throne room was easy, for they each had a ring of invisibility. There he was: Lord Erip Mav, sitting on the king's throne, wearing the king's crown. There was another throne next to the king's throne and this puzzled them. There had not been a throne for a female royal since the death of the queen. Since the throne was empty, they paid it little mind. They crept toward the throne. Each man held a silver stake; these would be used to kill the Lord Erip Mav. He was powerful, so they had brought some garlic along just in case. They had crept around and were now in front of the throne. Suddenly, a black mist flowed around them, betraying their presence to the vampires. They grasped hands and tried to teleport, but they could not. All was lost.

Erip laughed, high, shrill, and cold. Soon there were dozens of other vampires in the chamber. The invisibility rings were ripped from their fingers and handed over to Erip Mav. Then the doors to the chamber opened.

Taylee, granddaughter to the king and sister of Penrod, came striding down toward them. But she was different. She was not fighting the vampires: they were bowing to her. Penrod and Maug were devastated. She had been turned. Then they realized she was leading a young man, nearly grown. He looked to be between the ages of twelve and fifteen. She strode past them and sat on the throne. They had heard rumors about a vampire queen. They hadn't realized it was Princess Taylee.

"My dear brother Penrod," Queen Taylee purred. "It took you long enough to arrive. I thought you would not be here to meet my son before he reached manhood. But here you are. And you do not disappoint. You have brought Maug. Are you here to kill us?" She laughed. Her laugh betrayed her madness. It was clear that she was enjoying her newly found power. She would not relinquish it without a fight. But, if she truly was a vampire she would not relinquish it at all. "You have been gone for nearly twenty years. Plotting and scheming and where has that brought you? It has brought you here. Come, brother dear, we are going down to the dungeons. My son needs to practice his transformation spells. And our king wants a word alone with Maug!" Penrod shuddered at his sister's newly bone-chilling cackle.

Two hefty vampires came up on either side of Penrod and grasped his arms, frog-marching him from the throne room. All of the other vampires left as well, leaving Maug alone. Alone with the Vampire King.

They stood there, looking long and hard into each other's eyes. Then Erip saw it, it was unmistakable. The glint in the eye. "I know it was you," said Erip. "Don't even try to deny it. You killed Cardolo." There was a pause. With as much contempt as he could muster Maug spat at Erip. It landed right on his forehead.

"Yes, I killed Cardolo. What of it?" shouted Maug. Erip paused, he had decided not to kill Maug. No, he was going to curse him. But to do so he needed Leecher.

Erip snapped his fingers and a yellow, sallow skinned vampire appeared next to him. The stench of rotting meat and death clung to this vampire. "Leecher, I want you to age this man by one hundred and fifty years. I want him to be able to think and move. But I also want you to sap his power," Erip snapped his fingers again, and a sapphire appeared. "I will hold his power in this sapphire. He is not worthy of it." Leecher said

"Are you certain My Lord? Why not turn him?" Erip was outraged

"**Enough!**" he shouted. His voice rang through the room.

Leecher cowered. "Yes My Lord." Leecher ran forward and grabbed one of Maug's wrists. He held out his hand for the sapphire and Erip handed it to him. Maug began to fight. He was nearly able to plunge his silver stake into Leecher's foot. Erip shouted and four hefty vampires ran into the hall. There was a struggle. Maug fought valiantly, injuring two of the vampires with his silver stake. In the end they won, each brute pinning one of Maug's limbs.

Leecher began to chant; it was a terrible sound. Soon a red cloud surrounded Leecher and he approached Maug. The cloud engulfed them both. Maug screamed as Leecher bit down on his wrist. Suddenly the red cloud flowed into Leecher. Before their very eyes Maug began to age. His once great limbs shriveled. Darkness seemed to surround him. Then, a misty substance began to pour from his mouth, his ears, his nose. It was more white than opaque and not quite see through. The substance flowed through Leecher into the sapphire. The sapphire darkened, almost turning black. It was done. Maug was powerless.

Erip had Maug taken to the dungeon. He sent out a decree to gather all of the cityfolk to the palace. He wanted them to come to him. In the morning he would decree the fate of Maug. Maug was now powerless, and he would make Maug a wanderer. This would be the end of Maug.

The next morning everyone was in the square. Erip was jubilant. He had caught all but one of the king's family, and he had broken Maug. "Heed my words, subjects." Erip loved the authority in his voice. "This is Maug, son of Salen. He is to be banished. He has been stripped of his power. Nobody is to be caught helping him. If you are caught helping him you will be put to death. He is no longer a symbol that you can rally around. He is a broken relic of your 'golden age'. He will live away from society." After this speech Erip walked inside. His chosen few would escort Maug to the forest. There he would be left to fend for himself.

Erip had given instructions to his chosen few to go to the other cities with the same declaration. Anyone caught assisting Maug would be put to death.

. . .

Erip Mav drew up preparations to visit an entrance to the netherworld. One did not always need portals. There were legends that there was an entrance down in the Caves of Margeth. He could not be sure but if the legends were true, it would simplify his plans greatly. He made all of the preparations. He left his wife in charge of the affairs of the kingdom. Then he departed for the Caves of Margeth. The caves were very far away and this expedition could take a long time. He had to be very careful. His projections indicated that this expedition would take at most six months. Being away from the kingdom so long was a daunting prospect.

He however trusted his wife. She would take care of everything while he was gone. He brought with him his trusted friend. This friend hated his real name, and preferred to be known only as Lightning. It was from Lightning that Erip had learned to manipulate electricity.

Lightning and Erip traveled far to the north. They went to the caves of the Margeth. They began to experiment with electricity and other things to open the caves. It took them some time to find success.

Chapter Four
Dissensions

Dissensions were spreading throughout the kingdom. Maug's banishment disturbed people greatly. The people had trusted him and his family. Maug's family had been close friends with the king's family for generations. Banishing Maug did not endear Erip to the people. They were concerned because this vampire was weaving all sorts of dark spells around their palace. He was also making changes to their kingdom.

However, what disturbed the people most of all was Taylee. She had been greatly loved by the people, gentle and kind. Then this vampire had turned her into something evil. He had transformed her into something like him. Something that craved blood. It was terrifying. If Taylee could be turned to that, then none of them were safe.

There was a young man who saw this as an opportunity. To rally people to his cause. Or, to make rebellion his cause. His name was Chris. Chris was very unique among the people of the kingdom: he was were-kind. A were-wolf to be exact. He had only recently come of age and learned this fact. He had also learned that he was a fosterling. With his newly found powers he realized that he could make a huge difference in any efforts to overthrow the tyrannical government. But he was not sure where to go or how to do this.

Chris had the seeds of a plan. His adoptive father was a worker in the palace. If Chris could duplicate the keys, then he could sneak into the library. He knew that it was time to act. If he were to break into the library he might be able to access powerful weapons. Or maybe scrolls with powerful spells. He knew he could do it, but he wasn't sure if he *should*. Chris left the palace for a time. He needed to see what the rest of the kingdom was like.

Chris wandered the countryside. He would go into the cities and speak to men in pubs. He feared that there was nothing that he could do to help reinstate the rightful government. He was passable as a dog when in wolf form. He could also still read, and understand voices. He would go around listening in. Most people loved dogs so it didn't create any problems to wander into the inns and rooms to listen. This became a great advantage. But it appeared that nobody was willing to resist. He had heard nothing.

He traveled from city to city with no luck. He was beginning to feel very discouraged. He feared that nobody would be willing to stand up and rally to restore the rightful government. One day he found himself among wolves. He followed them home to their pack. They treated him with a sort of reverence. He sensed that they wanted him to follow them. So he did. He followed them to a cave. The cave was huge. They traveled deep into the cave. It must have been at least a mile. There, deep in the cave, was a fire. He approached the fire.

He saw a grizzled old man laying in front of a fire. The man rose; he wore a white fur cloak. An earthy aroma clung to him. He smelled like the forest, and also the musty smell of sweat and blood clung to him. Then the man spoke. His voice was like the forest. Like the roaring of a river and the howling of a wind.

"My son, you have returned. They named you Chris. That name suits you very well. Is it short for anything?" He said.

"Why do you call me son?" said Chris. The old man spoke again.

"My name is White-tail. I am your father. You were kidnapped as a child from my den. We searched for you but never found you. I know that you are my son, because like me you look like a dog when you are….transformed. Your siblings have been keeping watch over you since you left the palace," said White-tail. He looked at Chris.

"Yes, I do. And yes my name is short for Christian," said Chris.

White-tail nodded, "That makes sense. You should use your full name. It is more powerful. Now, we do not have a lot of time. I have a lot of heirs. You are a princeling to the throne of the were-kind. Magicians can sometimes transform themselves but not like us. You must use a copy of the key and break into the library. Do you understand?" Chris nodded.

"Why am I breaking into the library?" He asked White-tail.

"It is very simple. There is a prophecy there that you must take to Maug. Maug will be able to help you. Maug currently resides in his tree house in the forest. I will send your three brothers and four sisters to other cities to rally recruits. If they each bring ten men and women that should be enough. You must also bring some men and women to help you. When you return from your expedition I will be here waiting to help you. I will instruct them to meet you at Maug's treehouse in six months time. That will give you enough time to find the book and rally your own men and women. Also, take with you this ring. It is a ring of invisibility. Such artifacts come from another age. It will help you sneak into the palace, and remain undetected while you search for the book of prophecy. Do you understand?" Chris nodded. White-tail dismissed him.

White-tail sent two were-wolves with him to help. Red-fang and Gray-claw were very powerful and would help to protect him on the road, though they would not be able to enter cities with him. They were unmistakably were-wolves.

Chris made the long journey back to the main city. When he arrived there were whispers that Erip Mav had left for parts unknown. Chris was not sure what to make of this. But he was sure that it would be helpful. Somehow at least it would be helpful. He made his way back to his father's chambers in the palace. His father was not concerned about where he had been, but was grateful that he was home.

Chris made a copy of the key to the library. This was an arduous process. He had to learn how to molten the metal for the copy. He also had to learn how to make a mold. This task took a few months on its own. One day he was finally ready. He snuck into the palace and broke into the royal library.

The library was beautiful. He had truly never seen anything like it. There were hundreds of rows of books. There were ladders next to each row so that one could access the upper shelves. The shelves were marked according to their subjects. These occupied the walls to his right and his left. In front of him there was an empty space, hundreds of square feet. There were tables here for reading, and studying. Between the tables and the shelves were dark shapes. Chris shrank back, afraid that he had alerted vampires to his presence. He looked down. He was still invisible. He couldn't have been seen. As his eyes adjusted he realised what he was looking at.

He was staring at statues, thousands of them. There were statues of the gods and goddesses all over the library. They showed them sitting on thrones, fighting fearsome beasts, and forging terrifying weapons. He walked among the statues. There were also statues of the kings and queens. In an earlier age there had been dragons in the land. Here they were depicted in stone. The statues of the dragons were the most life-like. He climbed up onto the backs of the dragons. He pretended to be soaring through the air. He closed his eyes and imagined flying on the back of a dragon; even just in his imagination, it was exhilarating. He saw elves and fairies here. Some of the fairies were bigger than he was. He stood next to one. It was over six and a half feet tall. Tall fairy, he thought. He saw many were-kind depicted mid-transformation. There were also wolves, tigers, bears, lions, and hundreds of other animals here, cast from stone. There were dwarves forging weapons and mining gemstones. He stood alongside the dwarves and pretended to be striking the metal. The statues were glorious and wonderful. Truly they were a sight to behold. He wandered around in the library for hours simply staring at the statues, imitating their actions. Suddenly, the statue in the center of the room caught his eye.

It was a great dragon. Inscribed on the dragon's chest were the words *Take care that ye be pure of heart before you enter. Prove your worth to enter the room where the prophecies are kept. If you are worthy you may enter. If you pass the test you are allowed to take the item that you declare. If you are not worthy, then you will die within the room. Follow the instructions of the guardian Dragon to escape unscathed.* Chris thought that somehow he must enter the dragon statue. It was massive. Easily big enough to contain a room within it. He walked up to the dragon, and took off his ring.

The dragon stirred. Then it raised it's head and let out a roar that shook the ceiling. Chris panicked "Shhhh!" He cried "You'll disturb the rest of the palace and I will be caught." The dragon eyed him haughtily. The dragon spoke and it's voice grumbled like an earthquake.

"Fear not little were-wolf. My influence is only felt inside this room. No, I am not a true dragon. I am a living statue. Why do you seek access to the room of prophecy?"

Chris said, "Vampires have overrun the land and taken over the castle. I have come under the instruction of White-tail to seek the Book of Prophecies. There is a prophecy in it and instructions I am supposed to obtain." The dragon considered him. They stared into each other's eyes for a long time. Then the dragon spoke again.

"You are pure in heart. I will allow you entrance to the room of prophecies. But you must only take the third volume of the Book of Prophecies. The third volume contains the information that you need. If you attempt to remove more than this you will not be allowed to leave this room alive. Do you understand? There are other things in the room of prophecy. I am their guardian. Powerful spells, weapons, potions, potion books, the other volumes in the Book of Prophecies. You must not touch any of them. Do I have your word?" Chris nodded. The dragon moved his paws, and revealed a trap door. The dragon opened the trap door. The dragon said "Enter, and be quick."

Chris entered the room of prophecy. There was everything that the dragon statue had told him would be here and more. Things so powerful that they could not be spoken of. A ring of keys in a case with the inscription *These keys can open up portals anywhere, including the netherworld. Use them wisely.* That was a terrifying prospect. The netherworld is where the demons were locked up, or so said the legends. There were potions to kill with a single drop. There were books about magic and all kinds of other philosophies. Here were all of the things that he needed.

He felt a temptation to take as much as he could. There was something drawing him to the keys. The demons could overthrow vampires, couldn't they? That would be an easy way to restore the rightful government. He resisted the temptation. He was here for the Third Volume of the Book of Prophecies. It was the only thing that he was authorized to remove from this room. He took a deep breath and grounded himself. He focused with all of his might, only the book. He would only take the Third Volume of the Book of Prophecies. That's it.

After a few minutes of searching he located a shelf that read ***The Book of Prophecies***. He quickly took the Third Volume. He exited the room and went back up the stairs. The Dragon inspected him, content that he had only removed the Third Volume of the Book of Prophecies the dragon spoke. "You resisted strongly. Contained in this room are many secrets kept from the world. The fact that you resisted them says much about your character and your role in shaping the world to come. You should be proud. Very few could have resisted the temptation in the way that you did." After making this statement he allowed Chris to put his ring back on. The dragon resumed his original position, with his massive front feet covering the trap door. There was a feeling of powerful wind in the room. Then the dragon moved no more. Chris wasn't sure that he would believe that this had happened at all if he was not holding the Third Volume of the Book of Prophecies. It was such an interesting experience. Something that he was greatly intrigued by.

Chris went back to his family's chambers. He hid the book under his bed, under the loose stone he had discovered there years ago. Then he went to sleep. The living statue of the dragon wove in and out of his dreams. He wasn't sure what to make of it. Only a powerful enchanter could have created such a statue.

He awoke early the next morning. He removed the loose stone, and took out the book. He opened it but he could not read it. It was in an unfamiliar dialect. It was not written in common. He didn't know what language it was in. Hopefully Maug would be able to help him. He was greatly concerned. If the book could not be read how, then could they know the prophecy?

Chris decided it was time to recruit his men and women to follow him. Chris went around from inn to inn, and tavern to tavern. He did this for a month. But it wasn't working. Again Chris became discouraged.

Chris realized that he didn't even know how to go about recruiting men and women to join his fight. Properly it wasn't even his fight. But he had chosen to make it his fight. The words of his adoptive father seemed to echo around him though he wasn't here. Simple advice his father had given him. His father had said "Christian, if you want to know how people feel, you must listen. Listen more than you talk. Do not be obsessed with telling people everything you know, rather listen to what they can teach you. This will carry you much farther in life than your own knowledge ever could. Also, do not be obsessed with everything that you think you know. Focus on what you can learn. Learning is the key to success."

These were very wise words. He loved his adoptive father. The man had raised him and was incredibly wise. He had given all sorts of advice regarding a wide range of subjects. Most importantly he had taught Chris to think for himself. Being a free thinker was something that his father had stressed above all else.

Chris realized that he had to listen. He had to listen to what people were saying. This was the only way that he would be led to those who he could recruit. So this is what he did. He listened, and listened. He listened for six weeks. His time was nearly up. Two more months and he was supposed to meet up with his brothers and sisters at Maug's tree house. He didn't even know how to get to Maug's tree house. But he felt sure that a solution would present itself.

One night in a pub he saw two men sneak into a back room. He followed them, the door was locked. He heard men's voices. "I don't like the state of the government one bit! A vampire dictator! Ugh!" said one man.

A second man spoke. "That is all well and good, Johnny, but we need Maug. We cannot do this without Maug."

The first man spoke again. "Robert, I understand that we need Maug. But I promised never to reveal the location of the treehouse where we played as boys. So I will not."

Then a third voice spoke. This voice was that of a woman. She said "Robert, Johnny, I understand both of your points. Johnny, you must tell us where he is hiding so that we can seek him out. He is the only one who can help us. Isn't he?"

It was at this moment that Chris knew he should reveal himself. So he picked the lock and he entered the room. Immediately he was seized by rough hands and held firmly in place. There were two swift blows to his diaphragm. He was completely winded.

Then Johnny spoke. "What do we have here, a young vampire?" He produced a silver stake from within his robes. "We know how to handle vampires!" Then the woman spoke.

"Johnny, let him speak before you go making an accusation like that!" Johnny responded.

"Why should I, Kat? Answer me that?" Chris knew that there was only one thing for it. He transformed.

Everyone was dead silent. Chris morphed back into his human form and spoke "Will you listen to me now?"

Johnny put the silver stake back into his robes. "Well, aren't you just full of surprises," he said.

Chris began to speak. He told them of the plan that White-tail had outlined for them. He produced the book and none of them could read it either. There were twenty men and women in the room with him.

They all had much to discuss. After he explained the need that they all had — the need to overthrow the vampires — Chris was able to get them to trust him. They were all eager to start on their journey. They all pledged their lives to his cause. Johnny even agreed to lead them to Maug's tree house.

They put their affairs in order that night and left town. Before leaving, Chris left a note for his parents informing them of the journey that he had undertaken. He informed them to seek refuge with White-tail and help rally troops to the cause. Chris and his new friends met up outside the city that night and headed toward Maug's tree house. On the road they met up with Red-fang and Gray-claw. If all went well, they would arrive a few days before Chris's siblings.

Chapter Five
Maug The Hermit

Maug lived alone in his tree house. He hunted alone, he ate alone, he slept alone, he existed alone. Maug had been on his own for several months. He had been banished by the vampires. He sank into a wallow of depression and despair. He did not know what his purpose was any more. He was completely alone. His isolated existence was a result of the vampires who had overthrown the land.

Well, he wasn't completely alone. He had his forest friends. He could converse with animals, and sometimes even with rocks and trees. He knew that everything on the planet has a unique soul. This was something that his father had impressed upon him. He knew how to communicate with rocks, trees, and other animals very proficiently. He grew up hearing about fairies and elves as well, and occasionally dragons. But dragons were not often discussed.

He didn't have a favorite being. He did love birds though. He could name all the birds native to the area. They would help him to find nuts and berries. They even helped him cultivate his own garden. The birds and the beasts taught him how to plant. He had quite the garden cultivated.

Maug began to feel great depression. He missed his father and his friends. He had been unable to save them. He blamed himself. He began to engage in self destructive behavior. He would go days without eating or sleeping. His life was spiraling out of control. He began slicing tree branches with his sword. It was the only way that he could feel a semblance of control over his current predicament. He controlled how deep into the tree his blade went. This gave him a sense of control over his depressing life.

His life was so pointless. He had been unable to save his people, unable to save his father. Unable to accomplish anything. He wished that the vampire had turned him into a slug and left him in the dungeon with his friends. *As a slug that I would not be able to feel.* He would be able to just be.

Maug had grown tired of life. He began to grow pipe weed and drink alcohol. He believed that he could drown his problems away. Maug had opened his own brewery. Not that anyone would come to buy his alcohol, but it was a way for him to pass the time. Using magic he devised a way to make unnaturally potent alcohol. It was a powerful rum concoction, and he drank it far too much. It was only thanks to the tiny remnants of his magical power that he was able to hold off the liver damage.

. . .

A great river ran by Maug's tree house. The name of the river was Atlantis, named for a land far, far away. Down from the great mountain Olympia in the east, Atlantis flowed to the great ocean of the west. Atlantis was a mighty, powerful river, with many great sailing vessels upon it. There were many smaller streams and tributaries that fed this river. At its narrowest Atlantis was ten miles.

Great bridges had been constructed to get people across the river. They had gears and moving parts. They were called Steam

Bridges. They were able to rise to allow ships to pass. It was an ingenious structural engineering feat that allowed them to function and work in the way that they did. Steam would power great pistons, these pistons would crank and release, turning great wheels. Each bridge was composed of two drawbridges, powered by steam, one on either bank of the river. People loved their engineers. Their engineers were the only ones with the knowledge to maintain these bridges. The elves had invented these bridges and other wondrous things when they had lived in this land. When they departed millenia ago, they left the human engineers in charge of the bridges, giving them instructions on how to attend to them. The humans had maintained these bridges for all this time.

One day while staring at this river Maug decided that he wanted to sail away. He would sail down the river to the Great Ocean of the west. He would then live his days on the open sea. He would fish and live in isolation. He was already isolated. He didn't believe that he needed to stay alone in this tree house.

He thought that maybe he could meet a mermaid. Since the vampires took over mermaids had retreated from the rivers back to the sea. He had always had a strange attraction to mermaids. He missed them. So he began to build a ship.

He took his axe and began to fell trees. He was fast, he had the ability to move very quickly with magic artifacts, so he progressed much faster than average. He took massive trees to make his masts. His masts would run the whole depth of the ship. He worked, and he worked. Maug also had a little bit of magic left inside him. Just enough to help him make the ship powerful. Once the ship was done he would no longer have any of his powers remaining.

First he built the belly; it was magnificent. It took him a month to build the belly of his ship. There were rooms, and hammocks. He used a combination of woods and hand carved mermaids into the walls. The wood was very hard, but it floated, which was good. He did not build the ship after the manner of men, but rather after the manner of elves. He would occasionally sing to the wood in the language of the elves, using magic to shape the boat in the way that he wanted to. Elf magic was powerful, and while he was not an elf he could still shape the wood. Even though he had lost his powers the words of the elf language could still affect things, if ever so slightly. One of the purposes of singing to the wood was to triple its density, while also making it feather-light. Once built and completed, due to his songs this massive ship would be so light that it would only take ten men to move it.

Next, he worked on the mid-deck. The mid-deck needed to be sturdy. It is where the oars would be. He did not have men or women to move the oars, but it still felt right to build this part of the ship. He spent a lot of time on this area of the ship. He carved intricate statues into the railings. He hand carved beautiful benches for rowers. He also carved the oars. Again he did not carve the oars after the manner that was learned and taught by men, but he again copied the elves. Their long and elegant leaf shaped oars were far more powerful than human oars. There were twenty hand carved benches on each side of the ship, with room for three rowers per bench.

He also sang a unique song over each bench with a unique enchantment. Because his powers had been taken he had to use parts of an old wand as the source of power. It was the only wand he had. Now that he did not have full powers he could not wield the artifacts in his treehouse. Once he used it his minimal powers would be gone. On the center part of the ship, at the foot of each bench was carved a powerful creature. By the first benches there was a were-wolf carving. By the second benches there was a dragon carving. By the third benches there was a lion carved. By the fourth benches there was a phoenix carved. By the fifth benches there was a satyr carved. By the next benches there was a centaur carved. Then by the other benches elves, leopards, eagles, dogs, leviathans, elephants, sharks, foxes, a giant squid, owls, hawks, rinos, gorillas, and jaguars were carved . Maug could have chosen any twenty creatures, but he chose his favorites. The spell he wove was powerful. It allowed the individuals who sat at those benches to channel the power of those particular animals.

There is an ancient belief that life began with a single animal. It was believed to be a single cell. This belief was handed down to us from the gods. The gods also taught us that we could access these powers within ourselves and channel them. Creating powerful energy avatars, channeling powerful energy into our bodies, and many more applications besides this. He had created a very powerful boat. It took him several days to recover after creating these powerful benches.

Finally he added the upper deck. The captain's cabin was also added. He put an organ in the captain's cabin. He added the cockboat, the bowsprit, the quarter deck, the poop deck, the ballasti, and everything else that needed to be added to the upper deck. His ship was beautiful. He was ready to depart. He had plans to depart the next morning. He had used up what was left of his power. He only hoped that he would be able to escape. Without his power he would never be able to teleport or use magic again. He had used all that was left to build the boat.

It had been five long months since the vampires banished him. It had also been about twenty long years since the vampires had taken over. His ship was finished. He was going to sail off to the mermaids. He spent all day packing his vessel with essentials. He moved everything in his treehouse to the ship. He hid the most powerful magical items in secret compartments inside the captain's cabin. His cabin, he thought to himself. He packed his salted vegetables, and salted meats in the hold. He also brought his pots and pans into the ship. He brought his books, his weapons, and everything he owned into the ship. There was supposed to be a copy of a prophecy book here. Even though he searched and searched, he could not find it. Then he returned to his treehouse and went to sleep.

The next day a young woman came to his treehouse. He awoke with her singing to his plants. He came outside and asked, "Who are you?"

She spoke with a lilting cadence, her voice was beautiful and captivating. She said, "I am here to help prepare you. You have a great destiny ahead of you. You cannot run from your destiny."

"I can run from anything I want," scoffed Maug. He didn't know who this woman was to come here and tell him what he could and could not do. He was very frustrated. "I am leaving today!" he shouted.

She laughed, and her laugh was like the tinkle of a small waterfall. "You're going to leave in that?" She asked. She had frozen the water around his ship with a spell. His ship would not go anywhere until she chose to thaw it. He did not have the power to thaw it; after he had been drained by Leecher he lost almost all his powers. And what remained of his power after the vampire had taken it was spent. He was now nothing more than an old man, for the vampire had also aged him.

She began to cook and clean for him. She would help him to hunt. She would not leave him alone. He awoke to hear her singing to his plants every morning, just as on the first morning that they had met. He was a drunk wreck when she arrived. She began to nurse him back to health. He asked her name. She refused to give her name, and she had come to keep him company. She would sing to him, playing his bardic instruments. Whenever he asked her name, her response was always, "Soon, soon you will know my true identity." The woman was mysterious.

Things like this went on for several days. Finally Maug lost his temper. He shouted "I demand that you release my ship and tell me who you are. NOW!"

"No." She said it in such a quiet voice it made him furious. He unsheathed his knife and threw it at her chest with all his might. She raised her hand, and the knife turned into a flower. She caught the flower.

Then she spoke again "I will not tolerate attempts to physically harm me!" Her voice shook him to his very core. He fell to his knees.

"Fine!" he shouted, then wilted. "Please tell me what is going on here!" he pleaded.

He began to weep. All of his fear and frustration came pouring out of him at this moment. He wept and wept. She walked forward, she took his hand in hers and pulled him to his feet. He looked her in the eye. She touched his cheek, and looked at him with such love and tenderness.

"What are you?" he gasped. She twirled in mid air, body shrinking and wings sprouting. Then her body grew again. She now stood before him, over six feet tall, with a pair of iridescent wings.

She said, "I grow tired of waiting. I am a fairy. Tomorrow your fate will be decided. Get some sleep, you will need it."

Chapter Six
Arrival

Maug dreamed of a great battle at the palace. The battle was horrendous and glorious. He could not tell which side was winning.

The battle was difficult to gauge. Then, from within the palace a giant bat flew forth. As the bat flew, the soldiers of the opposing side fled from before it. Great warriors, men and women fell to the soldier riding the bat. Red lightning crackled forth from his sword. With the lightning alone he slew thousands of warriors, and not just men and women. This was a battle for the entire world. Creatures were fighting on both sides. The side that fought with the bat rider were mostly vampires.

Death and destruction rained, the bat and his vampires gained the upper hand. Slowly, painfully slowly they began to surround those that opposed them. Eventually they were surrounded on all sides. The battle was over. All was lost for the warriors and creatures of the opposition. Then, a portal opened up, and out came dragons, elves, fairies, satyrs, centaurs, and other creatures. Thousands of them poured from the portal. Then, the last creature to emerge was a purple dragon, ridden by a silver haired man.

Maug awoke with a start. He was breathing heavily and covered in a sheen of sweat. He didn't know what he had just witnessed. Something told him it may have been a foray of sight into events of the future. He arose from his bed and went to his window. The fairy was still there. She sat, singing to his plants, making them grow into various shapes.

He sighed. She was beautiful. She was exquisite and exotic. She was kind and patient, she was loving and compassionate. She was strong and powerful. She could do things he had only heard about in stories. One day, when she was bored, she sang to a tree until it was over one thousand feet tall. Sadly, it was forbidden for those who lost their magic, or had no magic, to pursue magical creatures for union. Besides, why would she be interested in him?

There was nothing he could do to woo her without his powers. He sat there wishing for his powers.

He was sad and depressed. He didn't know what he was going to do. Ugh, this fairy! Who did she think she was, coming here and giving him hope in a destiny that could no longer exist. He stared at his bed. He became lost in thoughts about what may have been. Then he heard the sound of many people walking toward his tree house. He exited his tree house. Walking toward him was a group of about one hundred people. At their head was a blonde haired boy. Maug stared around at them all. "What are you all doing here?" he asked. He had calmed down quite a bit but he was beginning to become agitated again. Didn't they know that they were risking their lives by coming here to try to help him?

Maug looked around. He did not recognize any of these faces. They were old and young. There were men and women. He thought about what it would take to help restore the rightful kingdom. Words that his father had spoken to him echoed to him through the years "Maug, people love their freedom. If anyone ever tries to take it all sorts of people will band together to restore the freedom of the people. If such a thing ever happens in your lifetime I expect you to be leading the charge to restore the freedom of the people. As the heir to the position of Captain of The Guard it is your duty. As one who knows how people are supposed to be treated it is your duty. I expect it of you. You have a great destiny, my son."

Maug began to feel a tingling in the tips of his fingers and toes. Suddenly his eyes lit with the fire of power. His countenance glowed, he looked happy. Then he laughed, he laughed out loud. He said, "With all of us here we can finally set forth on a proper expedition to find the rightful prince. Unfortunately I do not know where to look for him. We must put everything in order. We must also gather the creatures who will join us to fight this evil."

The boy replied, "It is already being handled. White-tail, the leader of the were-kind, is gathering them and other creatures to join us in a battle when the time is right."

Maug nodded. He began to speak with the strangers. He learned their names, and where they came from. Most of them were displaced farmers, but some were proper soldiers. Ten of them including the strange boy who appeared to lead them were were-wolves. This was excellent. Were-wolves were very powerful. They began to prepare.

All of their preparations began to come together. They put the newcomers' belongings on the ship. Then they laid out their plans. They knew that they needed to go to the east but they weren't sure where. Then the strange boy, whose name was Chris said, "Oh, I almost forgot. I have the Third Volume in the Book of Prophecy. Would that help?"

Chapter Seven
The Book, The Prophecy

"How did you get the Third Volume of the Book of Prophecy?" Maug asked Chris.

"I broke into the library of the castle and the Guardian Dragon allowed me to enter the room where it was kept." He elaborated on the tale of how he found the book. Everyone was in awe as he described the great library in the castle. "It is in a strange language that I cannot read. White-tail told me that you would be able to help me to read it." He said.

Maug nodded thoughtfully, "Well, I can give it a try." He took the book and opened it. At once it became apparent that he would not be able to read it at all. He turned to the strange woman who was with him "Well, my fairy, will you help us?" The woman nodded.

She took the book from Maug and opened it. "This is in high old Fae. The ancient and original dialect of my people. It will take me time to translate it into your language," she said.

Maug nodded, "That is fine. We must continue to plan."

. . .

Erip and Lightning were ensconced in a cave. They were searching for clues regarding the ability to open portals. They had been in this labyrinth for weeks with no success. They were considering leaving to go home. But they did not want to abandon their schemes so easily.

The maze was alive. Their awareness began when the maze began to move, they could sense it. The maze was aware of their thoughts and it moved. They also could not teleport out. Slowly, but surely the maze guided them to it's center. It was in the center of the maze that they were attacked.

They had found a series of statues, and when they tried to move past them the statues attacked. The statues moved and pinned them down. The vampires did not know what to do. They were nearly immortal, but great pain could still be inflicted upon them. Pain was something that they almost feared. The statues began to beat them. The statues threw them against the wall of the maze. The statues broke their bones and left them in a crumpled heap on the floor. Just before the statues could return to their plinths, Erip and Lightning threw lightning at the statues. The statues shattered. Erip and Lightning began to heal their wounds. It took them about an hour to heal themselves completely.

"Why did the statues break all the bones in our bodies?" asked Lightning. Erip groaned as he hit the floor several times to indicate that his jaw was still broken and he was unable to speak. A few minutes went by, Erip spat and blood splattered on the floor.

Erip said, "I imagine that it was some kind of test. If we were not able to heal ourselves then we would be stuck here. I imagine more powerful creatures like angels would be able to withstand the blows. But I am not sure. Those were powerful blows. Some of my bones were literally shattered. What about you, Lightning? Are you well?"

Lightning groaned "My whole body hurts. That's a new sensation. I don't remember feeling pain since before I was a vampire. Humans think that we vampires are invincible. I used to believe that too. All we really need to survive is blood. But today. Today changed how I feel. Today I think that we learned that there are certain enchantments that could very nearly kill us. That attack left us very broken, so broken that our wounds did not heal at their natural accelerated rate. What should have taken maybe a minute took us a full hour."

Erip nodded. He was very concerned. He wanted to know who had enchanted those statues. Whoever did it had to be a powerful, powerful sorcerer. Maybe even a dragon. He was not sure. This indicated to him that they were in the right place. Nobody would place such a powerful enchantment here for nothing. This must be the right place. He felt a strange presence here. Almost as if they were nearing a portal to the netherworld.

"Lightning, do you feel it? That odd tingling, pulling sensation?" Erip asked.

"Yes," said Lightning. "The closer I approach the archway the more powerful it becomes. It is strange, almost as if a powerful artifact is here. What if it is a trap, Erip? What if we go through the archway and we become trapped by powerful enchantments? We brought nobody else with us, and for good reason. I fear that anyone else, save Cardolo, would have died. But it is also a disadvantage. Yes, our people know our general location. But would they have been able to navigate the maze? I am uncertain that they would have been able to. Do we really dare continue?"

Erip paused. He was having similar thoughts, but as the leader he could not appear weak so he had not voiced them. He was very concerned that this could be a trap. Time was precious. They had been gone for such a long time. He trusted the other vampires, but he did not know what mischief the humans had been up to in his absence. This also concerned him. He did not know what was going on in the rest of the kingdom. His seeing stone wasn't working in the cave. It allowed him to communicate with anyone anywhere. He hadn't heard from his wife or son in weeks. He was deeply worried about them. He did not know what to do. This was a new feeling for him. He did know that what he sought was in the center of this maze, and the central chamber was just ahead.

"Lightning, I know that what we seek is in the center of this maze. If we do not go into this chamber beyond we may never leave these caverns. I think we have no choice but to go on," said Erip.

Lightning nodded, "So be it." With that, together they walked past the shattered statues and into the center of the maze.

. . .

Maug groaned. They had reached a hiccup in their preparations. Many of the people wanted to travel the river system and gather more recruits along the way. Maug disagreed. He found himself in a rather heated discussion with Chris.

"If we go around and gather troops to our cause it will do great things for us. Furthermore, a group of one hundred and two people is not big enough. At least I do not think that it is," said Chris.

"I know that our group is not that large. But consider, there are ten werewolves. Werewolves are very powerful. Also time is of the essence. If we are not careful then we will face opposition before we reach the Great Ocean. If we are attacked on the river Atlantis I do not know if we would survive. Consider this, we have hundreds of leagues to travel. All here understand the risks. The more people we recruit the more people whose lives will be at risk. Do you really want that on your conscience?" Maug nearly shouted.

Chris paused, Maug did have him there. He did not know if he could handle people dying on his watch. He just did know. "But we don't even know if we need to go to the Great Ocean or not," said Chris.

"Actually we do," said the fairy.

"You have completed your translation?" asked Maug excitedly.

"I have," said the fairy. "But I do not know if you will like it."

"What do you mean?" asked Chris. She held it out to the two men

"Here, read it for yourselves."

There will come a day of darkness. A day when vampires and other bloodthirsty creatures infest the land. The vampire leader will call himself Erip Mav. He is an ancient vampire. He is very powerful and he is thousands of years old. We have seen the boy who can defeat him. Before we tell you about the boy you must know about the plans of the vampire. He has been communicating through a seeing stone with some demons in the netherworld. He has agreed to release these demons if they help him to conquer our world and other worlds.

Please know that it is not just our world at stake. There are thousands of worlds at stake. It is down to you who are reading this prophecy to help save them. Trillions of innocent and free souls are counting on you. You must not fail them. Fear not, we will give you all the tools that you need to succeed.

Prophecy is not an exact art. The future is in flux, the movement of one grain of sand here on this world can affect the lives of billions of people elsewhere. So conversely can the lives of billions of people elsewhere affect a grain of sand here on this world. Even those of us who can peer through time do not always understand what we see. We simply record it, and hope that our scarier prophecies will not come to pass. In the event that they do, we attempt to impart to you in the future the tools you need to save the worlds.

First, you will need to find Maug. He is a very powerful man who will be able to help you. Next, you will need to find Christian, son of the Were-King White-tail. Once you have found them, you are ready to begin your expedition to find the other two most important people that you will need. You must travel by boat, along the river Atlantis to the Great Western Ocean. There you will find merfolk. They will be able to guide you through some of the more treacherous parts of the sea to the land of the fairies. The fairies will not trust outsiders in your time. Particularly humans.

Humans are susceptible to the temptations of great evil. You will need to convince the fairies to trust you. The fairies will then lead you to the elves. The elves are strange folk. They will have forgotten many of the strange customs of humans in your time. Do not despair. You must gain the trust of the elves.

It is paramount that you gain the trust of the elves because they will lead you to Carlos. The Silver haired Boy. He is the one you seek. Without him and his purple dragon Amethysta there is no hope for the free peoples everywhere. He is the first dragon rider in over ten thousand years. He will usher in a new era of peace. At least, that is the positive outcome we can see. The journey will be treacherous,and dangerous beyond imagination. Many adventurers will die before you reach your journey's end and find Carlos the rider of the purple dragon. You must not despair.

If you do not embark on this journey, great evil will hold this land for millions of years to come. Trillions of people throughout the known worlds will be enslaved. If you fail, it will mean failure for all worlds. Dark vapor will cover the lands, children will be stripped from their mothers to either become food for demons, or transformed into lesser demons. Vampires will have free reign. There will be great horror. The stuff of nightmares will be an everyday reality for most people. Those who are not killed will live as slaves to service the every whim of the demons. Death, destruction, darkness, these will be the reality. Creatures of light will all be killed or banished. Those who are not killed or banished will be corrupted into hideous shadows of their true selves. Fear, fear will be a daily feeling for people. Light will never abide in the known worlds again. If you do not embark on your journey, you will condemn thousands of worlds to darkness, destruction, and death. Darkness will reign, and when it does no one will find peace.

We know that this is a scary prospect. We long debated whether or not to record this prophecy for the fear that it would cause. We were concerned that if we recorded this prophecy that it would become self fulfilling. We were afraid that we would lead you to inaction, and your inaction would lead to the darkness that we have foreseen.

The gift of foresight is not perfect. As we have said, the future is in flux. We give you this one hope: within everyone is the ability to naturally dispel darkness from within. You must embark; we are forbidden to write about who you should take with you. We remind you that the future is very much in flux. Anything can happen. We foresee great things from all of you.

Also, we have seen the futures. We do not know which future will come to pass. We cannot stress enough to you that the future is in flux. The future shifts, and changes. You must be aware of this. You must know that our prophecies could be vastly wrong. But we are wise. In a sense we have traveled millions of years, in millions of years of seeing the future and recording our prophecies we have never seen, or in other words "met" someone who is not of value. Remember that you are unique. You are all unique and special. You can be successful. Do not fear the future, only believe in yourself. Good luck in your journeys. May the light and hope be with you always. May you vanquish all of your foes.

Do not read beyond this point unless you are unable to find Carlos.

There was nothing written beyond this point. "Didn't you continue to translate? It could have been important," said Christian.

"You betray your youth. Before all else fails, follow the instructions, Christian. Remember this," said Maug. Maug turned to the fairy, "I think that we should keep this to ourselves for now." The fairy nodded.

"I agree," she said. They turned to Christian.

"What do you think?" they both asked in unison.

"As you have pointed out, I am the young one here. I agree with both of you. I will defer to your judgment, and if I have a problem with it I will voice it," said Christian. Since his name had appeared so blatantly in the prophecy Christian had decided to use his full name.

"Good, now that that is settled we must embark on our journey," said Maug.

. . .

Erip and Lightning walked through the arch. They were not prepared for what they had found. They were in a room that was black. So black in fact that they could not see more than one foot ahead, and no matter what they did, the room remained black. They paused. If they turned around they could see the corridor from whence they had come. They were faced with a choice, they could either press on or they could turn back. They looked at each other. "Shall we press on, My Lord?"

"We must."

No sooner had Erip said this than a voice spoke. The voice was deep and powerful, so deep that it seemed to vibrate within them. It said, "So, two little vampires have come to ferret out my secrets. Tell me, little vampires, why I shouldn't eat you. You are pathetic blood sucking creatures and you do not deserve to live. You are evil vile creatures who seek to take life and freedom from others. Yet you are actually quite weak. You cannot face dragons without your flying steeds. You are strange, you sap life from everything around you. Even though your darkness is inescapable, you are puny. I may not even eat you. I may simply reduce you to dust. You are… Words cannot describe how insignificant you are. Tell me one thing, why should I let you live?"

Erip froze, he was familiar with things like this. It was a test of sorts. He wasn't sure how it was supposed to work, or in other words he did not know how to pass this test. However, he had to try to pass this test; his goals depended on it. What was it that his father had said to him all those years ago? The words echoed back to him, "My son, there are many tests for our kind in this world. Some of them are simple, others are hard, and some can be passed simply by challenging the person attempting to test you." He wondered if this test could be that simple. If all he had to do was challenge.

"Who are you to have this power? Who are you to be able to kill us with impunity? I demand that you name yourself!" said

Erip. There was a great rumbling and shaking. Then, the voice laughed. The laugh shook the room. There was a flash. Then the vapor turned red, then orange, then yellow, green, blue, indigo, purple. Then the vapor turned white as snow. There was a bright flash, and suddenly the vapor vanished. Words appeared before them in mid air. **You have passed this test. You are worthy to proceed. Use the stairs.**

"What does that mean?" asked Lightning. Boom! The floor below them began to shift. Soon they could see a stairwell that wound down, and out of sight.

"Well, let us go on," said Erip. They descended the stairs and found themselves in a room. The room was massive, and in the center of the room there was a plinth. Something was wrong, there should have been a guardian. Or, had they already passed the guardian and because of their challenge they were allowed to pass? This place was all wrong. This labyrinth had stood for millennia. It served as a way to protect the secrets of demon-kind, or rather how to gain access to demon-kind.

The keys that could open up portals to anywhere. They should be here. They had been made by the king of the dragons himself. He had removed seven of his scales. One from each color of the rainbow. He had carved each of these seven scales into a key. These keys were enchanted.

They walked to the plinth, and saw a note. The note read "Hello there! I have removed the artifact you are seeking. I speak, of course, of the keys to open portals to the netherworld. These keys can now be found at the palace. Within the room of prophecy. Without the keys to open up a portal you are probably wondering how you can get out of here. You were foolish to come here, but fear not. I have created a way for you to get home. I have placed a powerful enchantment on the plinth. Slap your palm down on the plinth and you will be transported outside the cave. Happy travels."

Erip roared with frustration. He was so angry! After all of their traveling only to discover that they had to return to the palace. He was more than angry, he was furious. He and Lightning slapped their palms down on the plinth and were transported out of the cave to the valley. Erip pulled out his seeing stone to contact his wife.

Erip imagined his wife and she appeared in the stone. "My beloved!" exclaimed Taylee. "Oh, how I have missed you. You have been gone so long, we began to fear the worst. There are strange things happening here in the kingdom. I have reports that there have been people gathering around Maug's tree house. There are currently over one hundred people there. I know you decreed that anyone who helps Maug was to be killed. I wanted to wait. I assumed you would want to deal with this yourself, my beloved. Oh, how we have missed you. I have been so lonely. Shall I dispatch troops to meet up with you at the tree house?"

Maug was very concerned. He did not know how to deal with this new development. He did know that he needed to act soon. Finally he asked "Do you know how they intend to travel?" Taylee paused, obviously conferring with an unseen person.

"It appears that they will be traveling by ship, my husband. Maug has built himself quite a large craft after the fashion of the elves. With a crew of one hundred people he could make it far. Perhaps even to the Great Ocean. If they are not traveling by ship then much is unclear. I am not sure why he would build such a large ship if he did not intend to use it. I am unfamiliar with nautical combat. What would you suggest?" she replied.

He pondered this for a moment. Finally he decided on a course of action. "Create a blockade of ships at the part of the river nearest to the palace. Nobody, and I mean nobody, is to be allowed to pass. I will teleport to the port city of Lauren which is nearest. We will take a sprinter class vessel down the river Kenan to the river Atlantis and meet up with the blockade. Have Leecher come. I want to taunt Maug with the sapphire containing his powers. I leave the proper preparations in your hands, my beloved," said Erip. His wife bowed, blew him a kiss, and then walked out of his range of vision. He placed the stone back into his pocket. They had to hurry to the city of Lauren and get on a sprinter class vessel. Lightning had heard all of his plans and preparations. He was fine with this. Erip nodded at Lightning, and he said "If you summon a lightning bolt I can use the energy to transport us to Lauren without wasting too much energy. Will that work for you?"

Lightning nodded. He held his hands up to the sky and summoned a bolt of white lightning that struck Erip. He grabbed Erip's hand and before the thunder boomed they were gone.

. . .

Chapter Eight
The Plan to Find Carlos

Maug and his companions put together their final preparations. They had finally agreed upon a course of action. They would set sail soon. They had decided to share the most relevant parts of the prophecy with their companions. But they had elected to leave their names out of it. Both Maug and Christian were greatly disturbed to see their names in prophecy.

Their plan was a simple one. They had argued long and hard about what to do. They had finally come to a decision. They would travel west, along the river Atlantis to the sea. From there they would search for mermaids in the Great Ocean. The mermaids would have to guide them to the Isle of the Elves.

Maug's ship was magnificent and would carry them wherever they needed to go. The ship was going on its maiden voyage and he had yet to give it a name. He counseled with his new friends.

"Well Maug," said Gray-claw. "What if we name it after you? We could call it Maug's Bounty." Nobody was very fond of this idea. So they continued to debate what the name of the ship should be. They spent long hours discussing the possibilities.

Then one day they came to a realization. It was so simple, and frustratingly obvious. Yet it had taken them so long to arrive at this conclusion.

"We are on an expedition to find a purple dragon. Wouldn't it be fitting if we named our vessel 'The Purple Dragon'?" said Red-fang. So they put it to a vote. The decision was unanimous. They all agreed to name their vessel The Purple Dragon. The Purple Dragon: the very name had a certain power about it. The Purple Dragon. They all wondered what the real Purple Dragon would be like when they met him or her.

"If we are to name our vessel The Purple Dragon then it should look the part," said the fairy. She began to chant. The strange sounds of the Fae language rang through the air. Tendrils of energy flowed around her and converged on the ship. The ship began to glow, dimly at first and then it grew brighter and brighter. When her chanting reached its peak there was a flash of purple light, and everyone was in awe of what she had accomplished.

The ship was now encased in a hard, translucent purple material. The entire bow of the ship was a great roaring dragon's head and rearing neck. The twelve foot long neck was capped with a great head larger than two horses. The scales on the dragon statue's neck caught and bent the light, creating little rainbows. The entire ship was now brilliant, dazzling, and seemed to glow with a light all its own. The stern of the ship was now a great ten foot long dragon's tail. The entire dragon head, neck, and tail were made of the same hardwood as the ship, but also encased in the same hard purple material as the ship itself was.

"My lady!" Exclaimed Maug. "What is this you have wrought? It is magnificent." He sputtered himself into silence. He was beside himself with wonder.

"Allow me to explain," said the fairy. "This craft will now be more than half again as fast. You will find a hole in the back of the dragon's neck, in the top of the dragon's head, and in her ears. If you pour oil into her ears, strike fire into the top of her head, and put bellows into the hole of her neck and pump, then this dragon head can breath white hot fire for thirty feet in front of the ship. The purple material that encases the ship is celestial iron. The metal of the gods. It is impenetrable. Only a weapon made of celestial iron can cause damage to it in any way. You will also find a seeing glass in the crow's nest that can see for over one thousand leagues if the proper adjustments are used on its dials. The masts have been made unbreakable. The sails are also likewise now enchanted. They will not tear except in enchanted weather, or under powerful attacks. I hope you are pleased with what I have wrought for you, my friends."

"Pleased?" said Maug. "Speaking only for myself I am ecstatic. Our vessel is now very formidable. We cannot help but to succeed in at least reaching the Great Ocean. Thank you so much for what you have done for us!"

"It is my pleasure," said the fairy and she bowed slightly. Their preparations for departure began to come together.

Then they began to argue again. They again could not decide what to do and their plan was falling apart. They had many arguments. It was not until the next day that how bad things were became apparent.

"I'll show you an idiot!" shouted Mason. The shout woke Maug. He came out to find Mason advancing on Christian. He began to strike Christian. He struck him over and over again. Christian was soon bleeding, he allowed each blow to land. The next time Mason tried to strike him he leaned back and transformed, then he leaned forward and struck back with his paw. He drew four great scratches across Mason's face and sent him sprawling into the dirt. Mason drew forth his sword and advanced again. As he went to strike Christian, Maug sprung between them.

"What do you think you are doing!?" Maug shouted and everyone that was still asleep came running. "Why on earth are you fighting!? By the gods this will get us nowhere! Again I ask you, what are you doing?" There was a great anger in his voice. Had he still possessed his powers the entire ground would have shaken. As it was, the people still shook from the anger in his voice.

"He called my plan stupid!" shouted Mason. "All I want to do is gather more recruits. One hundred and two people is not enough to wage a war. I say that we wait here and gather a few hundred more people to follow us. Maybe even a few more ships too."

"Mason, we have already covered this," said the fairy calmly. She walked over and began to heal him. "Our best chance is to leave now. As Christian has told us, Lord Erip Mav has gone exploring the caves to the north. Now may be our only chance to leave. After what I have done to our vessel we will not leave undetected. We will be seen, and Erip Mav will most certainly be told where we are. We must leave now. Otherwise I fear all may be lost. Now, apologize to Christian," she said, "And Christian, apologize to Mason."

The two of them begrudgingly apologized to each other. They again began to discuss their plan. When they all reminded Mason that he could stay behind he sobered up quite a bit.

"I apologize for my earlier behavior. I acted very rashly. Christian, please accept my apology. I will try to do better in the future," said Mason.

"I accept your apology," said Christian "Now that we are getting along again I would remind you all of the prophecy. We have a mission to accomplish. Let us go and accomplish this mission. Let us travel to the land of the fairies and the elves and gather an army more powerful than anyone has seen in living memory. Let us gather the dragons. Let us gather an army that will help us fight for FREEDOM!"

They all shouted in unison "FREEDOM!" over one hundred voices, a clarion call. Based on their discussion, White-tail would rally what free humans he could and the dwarves. White-tail would also send an expedition to the east, where the centaurs and satyrs dwelt. White-tail had vowed to travel even further east to the land of the unicorns. They would all gather again in this land to decide the fate of the worlds. It would take time for the old wounds to be healed. They needed to establish ties with all the races once again. They needed to communicate and plan. If all the races of light had been in communication, nothing like this would ever have happened. Many would die, but their sacrifices would be noble. Many would die, so that trillions could live.

They had finally agreed on a plan. They would follow the advice of the prophecy. They would travel down the River Atlantis. They would then travel into the Great Ocean, and seek the mermaids. Then they would follow the advice of the mermaids to find the fairies.

Finally they were ready to depart. They all went into their ship and began their journey down the River Atlantis.

. . .

Erip and Lightning arrived at the city of Lauren. There was a feast prepared in their honor. The dishes all involved blood. Blood whiskey, blood pudding, blood chicken, blood bread, and many more besides. They enjoyed the feast greatly and gorged themselves on the dishes available.

It took a few days to prepare a crew for the sprinter class vessel. They all had to be strong warriors. They were of course humans, the vampires' preferred slaves were always human. Humans may be a weak and inferior race but they would serve the purpose of Erip.

"My Lord," a man approached Erip and bowed. "The sprinter vessel is ready, My Lord. Would you care to enter it and have us depart?" Erip paused. He sensed a great disturbance. He pulled out his seeing stone, and was greatly disturbed by what he saw.

Near a tree house there were over one hundred people. They were entering a fantastic vessel that looked almost like a dragon. Lord Erip Mav screamed. "They have a head start. Take me to the sprinter class vessel NOW!"

Erip Mav was escorted to the sprinter class vessel where he entered it. They took off. They were flying down the river. Almost literally flying, with the aid of Erip Mav's magic. Erip Mav was determined to rendezvous with his fleet before the strange dragon ship arrived. He would break Maug by taunting him with the gem that held his power. He would then claim that strange vessel for himself.

Erip walked along this ship. The human captain came scurrying toward him. He was a short man, barely four feet tall. *He must have some dwarfish blood in him*, Erip thought. The man had a long beard that reached his waist. His beard was braided with beads and feathers. This strengthened Erip's suspicions that this man was descended from the dwarves. Despite his diminutive size this man was very strong. One more odd observation that Erip was able to make was that the man was bald on the top of his head. Then the man spoke.

"I am Captain Ularth, My Lord. I have come to escort you to your cabin." His voice squeaked.

"My cabin? Did they not inform you? While I am a guest on board your vessel I will occupy your cabin," said Erip Mav.

"My Lord I am sure that you will-" began Ularth. Erip Cut him off.

"Would you dare to contradict my wishes? I will sleep in your cabin or I will have you thrown off this ship!" snarled Erip.

"Yee-es, yes, yes of course, My Lord" Squeaked Ularth. He began to tremble and Erip laughed again.

"Well then, take me to *my* cabin," shouted Erip. Ularth bowed, and led Erip to his own cabin that Erip would be occupying.

Erip spent his time in the cabin strategizing what would happen once they rendezvoused with the rest of the fleet. He would have his men prepare ballasti and great vats of oil. He would have hundreds of ships create a great blockade. Nothing would get past them on the river.

Then there was Maug. He was a shell of the great warrior he had once been. Erip would torture Maug. He began to ponder this. Perhaps his advisors had been right about Maug. Perhaps he simply should have killed him. No! He thought to himself. He was the great Lord Erip Mav. He had killed the king. He would not let others cause him to second guess himself. Still he began to wonder. What was the point of all this? Yes, ruling the many worlds that legend spoke of would be fun, and he would leave a great legacy behind for his son. Yes, he did enjoy torturing and killing. Yet those who resisted him, they did it with such a strength and determination, and he was uncertain what to make of it. He feared it. It interfered with his meditations, and his powers.

"NO!" he snarled. He would not allow such thoughts to plague him. He was on the right course of action. He would free the demons. He would create a world where dark and fallen creatures could live in happiness doing what they loved.

Again he paused. Was it really happiness though? Ugh, where were these thoughts coming from? He pulled out his seeing stone. About one thousand years ago, when his father had given him the seeing stone, he had given advice as well.

"My son, the seeing stone is powerful. Remember that powerful beings can reach out and touch the stone. They can access your mind through the stone. You must guard against such influences. If you do not, you will be destroyed by these powerful beings. They seek to destroy all dark and fallen creatures. They would wipe us all from existence. We do not fall into their paradigms. So they seek to wipe us out. Be wary of them," his father had said.

Unbidden, unwanted he heard a voice in his mind. "We do not seek to destroy you. We seek to heal you. All dark and fallen creatures were like us once. We seek to heal you."

"No! Be gone from my mind!" He threw up impenetrable barriers to his consciousness. He did not want to be influenced by those powerful beings his father warned him about. The existence of dark creatures was a grand existence. They did not need to be healed. Erip had never before been contacted by one of those beings, and while it did not happen again he was greatly disturbed by it.

While Erip was by himself in the cabin, Lightning was wandering the ship, torturing the men on board for his own pleasure. Simply being around him was a torture. So he would disguise himself, jumping out when they least expected him to. He was greatly amused by this. Occasionally he would provide a small shock to them. They would scream and Lightning enjoyed hearing their screams. He would roar with laughter every time he made one of them scream. He enjoyed this voyage very much.

Time went on like this for several days, Erip ensconced in the captain's cabin, and Lightning running around the ship scaring the pants off of people. In some cases literally. When they neared the great port south of the main city Erip exited the cabin.

"My Lord," said Ularth. "We have arrived at the main port. Are you ready to depart?" Again his voice was squeaking. Erip loathed him.

"Yes!" snarled Erip. "Lightning and I shall depart." With that they left the ship. Erip hated being onboard that ship. It had been pathetic. At least the humans in the palace were able to hide their fear. It made them much easier to deal with.

"Lightning, bring me all the generals and admirals. Bring them here to this very spot. Ships should be coming up and down the river. We must catch them here. If they escape, our plans to open the netherworld will fail. We must establish the blockade and stop them. Bring the generals and admirals and we will begin to plan," said Erip. He sat himself down to wait for them to arrive.

. . .

Lightning left Erip to himself. Lightning was worried about his master. He was afraid that something strange had happened to him during the voyage here. He went into the city and found many of the admirals and generals waiting for him, along with the other men who would crew the nautical vessels. There were hundreds of thousands of soldiers, both human and vampire, and they told him twenty thousand ships waited only a little ways away up the river. This ambush would stop the rebellion in its tracks. Some of the men were of course humans, but a majority of them were vampires. Many humans had been turned while they overtook the land. There were now millions of vampires, and vampires outnumbered humans nearly two hundred to one.

Lightning was very concerned when he did not see Leecher. But then he saw him running toward them. Leecher had brought the sapphire. Erip would be pleased. They all returned to where Erip Mav was waiting to hear his plan.

. . .

They all arrived at the place where Erip Mav was waiting. Erip Mav had given up on claiming the Purple Dragon. He would destroy it and all on board instead. He outlined his plan. They would pour oil onto the water. Any ship that sailed through the oil would be saturated in it. Then they would light the oil ablaze. This oil had been specially enchanted to burn for long periods of time. Then, if their vessel somehow survived it would be attacked by thousands of larger vessels. These vessels were equipped with all of the best weaponry.

Including an old invention of the elves. These inventions were called cannons. They were large metal tubes, closed on one end. The other end was open, and was filled with a special powder and packed down with a large ball. This powder would be ignited through a hole in the top, near the closed end. This would burn the powder, creating a build up of pressure. This build up of pressure would send the ball flying out the open end of the tube. His men did not believe him that this device worked the way that he said. They had laughed and jeered as he had described it.

It was only right that they would laugh, he thought to himself. They were vampires all. They had never heard of such a thing as the steam bridges until they had conquered this land. Erip wondered what other secrets the elves had. Someday when he conquered the elves he would know all of their secrets.

Erip had kept them hidden from his men, so it was not entirely a surprise that they would not believe him. He had found a storage cave beneath the port containing millions of cannons. Barrels and barrels of the powder, and heaps and heaps of the balls.

He had only told the head admiral about them. The head admiral's name was Waterbeard. A strange name even for a vampire. Erip trusted him completely. Waterbeard and his nine brothers were the ten main Admirals of the fleet. Then there were Waterbeard's extended family. They made up the remaining captains and admirals of the fleet. They would guide the fleet in battle.

Waterbeard had begged Erip to allow him to tell the other captains and Erip had agreed. They had secretly spent months learning the secrets of the cannons. Now they were masters of the weapon. When the men said that they did not believe him, that was fine with Erip. He would show them.

"Bring me a cow," said Erip. Two vampires ran off toward the port and brought Erip a cow. Then he ordered Waterbeard to bring out a cannon. "Load the cannon and show our unbelieving friends here the truth of my words."

"Yes Erip," said Waterbeard. They left and brought a cannon. They instructed all of the men how to load it and fire it. Then they made a demonstration on the cow. They took the cannon hundreds of feet away, loaded it and fired.

The large black ball ripped a hole through the cow and kept on flying. The cow did not even have time to scream before it died. The men were astounded. Erip had the men train with the cannons until their speed pleased him. Then they began loading the ships with oil, cannons, gun powder, and the balls. Erip knew that the strange vessel that he had seen had leagues to travel, but still they had to hurry.

Erip was relieved when all of their preparations only took a few days. Their thousands of ships created a blockade on the river, and just in time too. For their scouts had come to warn them that a strange purple ship was approaching.

Chapter Nine
River Warfare

Weeks on the river had put Maug's mind somewhat at ease. He enjoyed the feeling of being on the water. The river was so large that some people considered it a small sea running through the land. But no, it was a river. It was a beautiful and deep river. Full of all sorts of mysteries. People had been exploring the river for centuries, but it still had secrets. Secrets it would hold until the end of time.

There were thousands of species of fish that lived in the river. All kinds of fowl that survived on its banks. There were great sharks in this river. And because of the river's size, there were rumours of something greater still.

Maug wanted to check on the progress that they were making, so he climbed up into the crow's nest.

"Anything to see up here, Seber?" Maug asked. Seber nodded. He looked grave. He silently passed the seeing glass to

Maug, pointing to the east as he did so. Maug looked to the west and was dumbfounded by what he saw.

He saw thousands of ships ahead of them. They were far away now, but they were unmistakably making a blockade to stop them from continuing on their voyage. They would have to fight hundreds upon hundreds of ships and they were but one vessel. Even with the improvements from the fairy, Maug was uncertain if they would be able to make it through.

"Keep us apprised, Seber. If they begin to travel towards us let us know. I will send someone else up here to be your messenger," said Maug. He descended the main mast and gathered the crew around him.

He explained to the crew the ships that were ahead of them, and how they were going to have to fight. They began to make all of their preparations.

"I wish I had my powers." Maug said to the fairy. "I would be able to help us greatly if I had them. I'm glad we have you."

"My powers are very weak after outfitting this ship. I will not be able to help much," the fairy said. Then she added with a twinkle in her eye, "Your powers may not be lost forever." She pulled out a white staff and handed it to Maug. "Take this staff. It has some unique powers of its own. When the time is right, use it wisely."

"Thank you," said Maug. He was grateful for everything that the fairy had done to help him, and also his friends. She would be a great ally to them in the days and months to come.

He often wondered about the fairy. In his moment of greatest need, when he was a drunken wreck, she had appeared to help him. Many questions occurred to him; where had she come from? What was her real name? How old was she? Who had sent her to help him? Why was she so beautiful?

These and many more questions about her occurred to him. He was uncertain what to do about his attraction to her. She was so stunningly beautiful. Yet again the conundrum about it being forbidden was brought to his mind. Ancient laws had been put in place by someone. Nobody knew who had put those laws in place. He was afraid of his forbidden feelings, and he was afraid of facing the fleet.

Day by day, hour by hour they came closer and closer to the ships that blockaded the river. They were all a little afraid. But they knew that they would be successful. Somehow they must be successful.

As they drew nearer to their enemies, a sense of foreboding entered the crew of The Purple Dragon. They had no doubt that they were all fearsome warriors. Yet, still they feared the battle that was imminently before them. Some of them had never seen battle before. They did not know what to do. More than half of them were not trained in nautical combat. Many were very young, and yet some were very old. There was little hope to go around. Again Maug wished for his powers back. With his powers he could destroy many ships at a time. He would be able to turn the tide of the battle.

For now at least his hopes would be in vain. Without the sapphire containing his powers he would not be able to restore them. He did not know if restoring his powers without killing Erip Mav was possible. But someday, he would try.

The day finally came when they arrived near the blockade. Erip Mav spoke to them in a magically enhanced voice.

"Surrender now! If you surrender and allow yourselves to become slaves to my regime I will spare your lives. We are ships of thousands. You are but one vessel. How can you hope to defend against us?!" cried Erip Mav.

As they got closer and closer they saw that the entire river was covered in ships. Bank to bank, one thousand ships wide and twenty ships deep. The bows and sterns of all the ships were touching.

"We are in very deep trouble!" cried Christian. He turned to Maug, "How can we hope to get past that?!" Christian was very afraid, it was clear. Many of the other people were afraid too.

Hardened warriors though they all were, this battle would test them all.

"Let us pass in peace. We merely wish to leave you to these lands and travel to the east. A place where you have no hold on the land. Let us pass and we will not touch your fleet," said Maug.

"No, you will not be allowed to pass." Erip Mav yelled back and he laughed. "You will all die! Attack!" He cried.

The battle began in earnest. Large black balls were hurled at the ship. As the ship was encased in Celestial Iron, the large black balls simply glanced off the sides of the ship.

"Light the oil!" cried Erip Mav. His men lit the oil. The oil licked the sides of the ship but it did nothing.

"What is going on?!" Erip cried to his captains. "Admiral Waterbeard, why are the balls fired from our formidable weapons having no effect?! Why is the fire not consuming that ship!? Tell ME!"

"My Lord, I have read about this in the cave where you found the cannons. The only material able to withstand the cannons is known as Celestial Iron. Where these rebels obtained Celestial Iron is beyond me," said Waterbeard. Celestial Iron, this would complicate things.

Suddenly the dragon head on the purple ship erupted with fire. The fire vaporized over one thousand ships in a few minutes. This was not a great loss to Erip's fleet. But as the battle continued he began to lose many ships.

Ballasti on the purple ship began firing. The ballasti were covered in pitch that was lit on fire. His fleet began to be consumed. Soon his fleet had been reduced from twenty thousand ships to about fifteen thousand. The fact that they were destroying the fleet Erip Mav had built over the last decade was very frustrating for him. Erip Mav did not know where they had gotten such a vessel but he wanted it for his very own.

Erip Mav whistled. A large bat, large enough to carry ten horses, erupted from the water in front of the purple ship, cutting off the tongue of flame. Erip jumped, and using magic carried himself up to the bat and alighted on its back.

"You see this sapphire Maug?" For Erip had pulled the Sapphire out of his robes. "This is your power that I stole from you. I will crush you now and take your ship. You will exist in my dungeon as a slug. Your loathsome rebellion will be crushed here and now. Who are you people to stand against me? I will conquer all the worlds. I will release demon-kind. I will rule over all lands, everywhere. Who are you to stand against me?"

"We are representatives of the free peoples of this land. We represent the free peoples of all lands. We would cast you down and restore the rightful prince to his throne. You have no claim on his throne. We would see you cast in irons for what you have done—" said Maug. Maug continued to speak, but Red-fang could no longer hear him.

Suddenly Red-fang had an idea. He ran below decks. He did not know if he still had it but he had to try. He ran to his hammock and began to search. He dug around, becoming discouraged when he did not find it.

Finally after several moments of searching he found the dragon scale that his father had given him when he came of age. It was said that dragon scales could undo powerful enchantments; it was also said that they had the power to kill dark creatures. Dragons did not often part with their scales. This scale was a family heirloom that had been handed down for centuries. He ran back up to the main deck of the ship. Quickly he tied the dragon scale to one of the javelins they used as projectiles to be fired by the ballisti. He loaded the javelin, lined it up with Erip Mav's bat. His plan was simple: kill the giant bat. He said a quick prayer to the gods and goddesses. Then he fired. Thwup! The javelin was away.

Erip Mav's bat had watched the javelin being launched and dove to avoid it. The bat did not dive quickly enough. The javelin connected with the large sapphire in Erip Mav's hand. There was a screeching sound, like when metal scraps against metal. And the sapphire exploded.

Then several things happened all at once. Erip Mav screamed, and Maug began to glow. Maug lifted his white staff.

"To me!" Maug shouted. And he laughed out loud. This was the first time that Maug had felt truly joyful since learning of his father's death. The white cloud that had come from the gem flowed from Erip Mav down to Maug. It swirled around him and he began to age backwards until he was as young and strong as he had been before Leecher had drained him. The glowing around him intensified until there was a bright flash of light.

Maug's powers had been restored. A powerful blast of energy shot forth from Maug. This energy caused about two thousand ships to sink, and threw Erip and his bat onto the northern shore of the river. This knocked out the bat, and Erip Mav.

There were still over thirteen thousand ships. They quickly surrounded the purple ship. It was all Maug could do to protect his friends from those great black balls that were being launched. They began to repel boarding parties. Soon there was fighting on The

Purple Dragon herself. The boarding parties had broken through. They were not killing. But they were definitely maiming people as they went. Maug began to despair again. He was afraid that they would be unable to fight the boarding parties off their ship. He was also afraid that he would be able to win past this fleet. In this moment of despair he thought of his father. And in that moment, Maug had a vision.

He was walking along a grassy field near his childhood home. There was a man walking toward him. The man looked young. Very young. As the man got closer Maug recognized his father.

"My son!" exclaimed Salen. "Oh how I have missed you. I look forward to our great reunion when you join me among the stars. Come tell me what is happening."

"Father, I am happy to see you. But I do not have time for this. I have to get back to the battle," said Maug.

"Oh my son, time passes differently here. You will return at exactly the moment you left. Please tell me what has happened," said Salen.

So Maug explained what had happened over the last few decades. He told his father of building up the rebellion. He told how they had gone to the south to get help from the dwarves. He told of betrayal at the hands of the dwarves. He told of how he had lost his powers and been banished. He told of how he had become a drunk, and drowned his problems in his alcohol. His father was disappointed by this, he could tell, but his father listened in silence. He told of building his ship, after the manner of the elves as Salen had taught him. He told his father of the fairy who had come and nursed him back to health. He told his father of the one hundred strangers who had shown up the next day. He told of the Third Volume of the Book of Prophecies. He told how his name and the name of the were-wolf Christian had been contained within the book. He told how the fairy had transformed their ship. He then told of their departure, and of their trip down the river Atlantis.

Then he told of the blockade. His father was very interested in this. Maug explained how he, by a happy accident, had just got back his powers.

"Now you know what has transpired. What would you suggest that I do?" asked Maug.

"My son, how quickly you turn to the easy way to get rid of your problems. No matter. You are of sober mind now. That is what matters. There are many things that I could tell you. But I would cast your mind back to your uncle Maurice," said Salen.

"Wasn't my uncle Maurice the crazy man who fell in love with a mermaid?" asked Maug. He had always been told not to listen to uncle Maurice. Uncle Maurice had always been discredited. People thought he was crazy. Nobody liked their children to spend much time around him for fear that he would teach them his strange beliefs. To hear his father talk about this man with reverence was disconcerting. Still, he kept his own counsel. He waited patiently for his father to explain.

"Yes, he was," said Salen. "And we were wrong to tell you not to listen to him. He may have been a little strange, but everyone has their oddities. Now, Maurice was of the philosophy that you should rely on animals and nature to help solve your problems," said Salen.

"I don't understand father, how can that be of any use to me now?" asked Maug. He was beginning to wonder if this was just a figment of his imagination.

"First, I am not a figment of your imagination. Second, can you not think how relying on animals and nature would be of help to you? Some things I cannot tell you. You must learn them for yourself," said Salen.

Maug thought. He was not altogether confident that this was not a figment of his imagination. Then he remembered the stories that he had heard as a young boy. Stories about fantastic beasts of the sea. Giant squids who could drag ships down to the depths of the water. Massive whales that could swallow a horse and rider whole, or so the stories said. Sharks large enough to *prey upon those whales and squids. Then there were the creatures that preyed on giant squids, whales, and sharks. The kraken, nobody was sure if there was only one kraken or many. The legends said that there were many. It was said that the kraken and these other creatures were pets of the sea gods. The kraken, or krakens, were supposedly large enough to swallow giant squids whole. There were two other creatures he remembered from the tales. Giant sea serpents known as Leviathans, who were supposedly large enough to swallow entire fleets of ships whole. Then there were hydras. Known as the kings of all the sea monsters. They were extraordinarily powerful. The hydra legends varied. Some say that the hydra only had 7 heads. Other legends say that a hydra is born with seven heads, but if you cut off one head two heads grow in its place. Meaning that a hydra that had seen battle could have thousands of heads or potentially millions of heads as the case may be. Maug looked up at his father. Salen was beaming.*

"You are nearly there," said Salen.

"You mean to tell me that all those legends about sea monsters are real? That krakens, giant squids, giant whales, giant sharks, leviathans, and even hydras are real?" exclaimed Maug. He could not believe it. He could not believe it! Those fantastical beasts of the sea were rumoured to be incredibly powerful. They could do things that men had only dreamed of. He did not know all the things that they could do.

"Why yes," said Salen, "And I can teach you how to call them for help."

"Wait, I can call on these creatures to help me?" inquired Maug. "I thought that they would attack all vessels."

"Millenia ago we forged peace with these creatures. They help guard our rivers from evil. The water is their kingdom. They ultimately serve the sea gods, but they will help you. It is very simple. You use your power and call out 'Brother or sister leviathan' or whichever creature you need the assistance of, you name your need and if they are willing they will come. If you *explain the direness of the situation they are far more likely to come to assist you. Do you understand?"*

"Yes father," said Maug. "There is one more thing." Maug did not want to give voice to this for fear of offending his father.

"You wish to know if this is real?" said Salen.

"Yes," said Maug.

"There are many strange things in this world, my son. From where I am, I have been allowed to reach out to you to help. This is very real. I love you, my son. Peace be with you. May you and your friends save the kingdom." There was so much more that Maug wanted to know. He did not want his father to leave him just yet. "I must go, my son. But remember, I will always be with you," said Salen. And slowly he faded away.

Maug collapsed on the deck of the ship. Christian rushed over to him. He helped Maug rise to his feet.

"I know what we have to do," said Maug. "I have to get in the water."

"Are you crazy?!" screamed Christian. "They are about to surround us, and you want to jump into the water?"

"Do you trust me?" asked Maug. It was a great moment. Absolute trust was something rarely bestowed in such turbulent times. Christian made a simple one word statement.

"Yes." Christian said.

Maug ran to the edge of the ship, staff in hand and jumped into the water. People came rushing toward Christian.

"Where did Maug go?!" they all cried in unison. There were varying degrees of concern on their faces.

"He had to do something to help. I do not know what," said Christian. Down in the water Maug was chanting.

"Brothers and sisters, creatures of the water, we need your help! There is an army upon us. They mean to stop us and enslave the universe. Even water dwellers such as yourselves will not be safe. You must help us please. Hydras, leviathans, and krakens I call upon you most specifically. You that are the scourges of fleets. We need your help to conquer these vessels and help us. Will you please help us? Will you please help us to win past these ships? We beg of you." Maug said all this and more to the creatures in the sea then he used magic to return to the ship.

"I have attempted to contact reinforcements from the sea. We will see if they come," panted Maug. They continued to battle the enemy fleet. Though they were able to fend off the boarding parties, and they were able to destroy many more ships, they were losing this battle. They began to fight like lions, never had men been known in that age to fight with such strength. Yet, Maug feared that it would not be enough.

Then the water began to roil. There was great bubbling and frothing taking place. It was as though the river itself had come alive. Then many heads broke the surface at once. The creatures spoke in unison. The ship shook, and their voices were like the sound of rushing water.

"You have sssumoned us to help you in an endeavor. We ansssswer you brother Maug. What would you have usss do to help you?" There were several creatures before them in the water. One of them looked to be a giant serpent with great fins. When it opened its mouth to speak its mouth was hundreds of feet wide. This was clearly a leviathan. Then there was a many headed beast, each head more than ten times as large as the dragon head on the front of their own ship. It was clearly a hydra. Then, there was a kraken with several arms and legs, it looked fearsome and deadly. Its hands were hundreds of feet wide.

"My brothers and sisters from the water. We need your help. Can you destroy the fleet before us?" Maug asked.

"Asss you asssk Maug. We ssshall destroy the entire fleet for you. It isss fortunate that the vampiresss have none of their creaturesss with them. If they had, thisss would be much more difficult. Asss it isss this should be simple for usss. Isss there anything elssse that you require from usss your brothersss and sssissstersss of the SSSEA?" The great creatures asked.

"No, but my companions and I thank you, our brothers and sisters of the sea. We are in your debt," said Maug.

"Sssomeday Maug, we will collect thisss debt from you," said the sea creatures.

The battle was fearsome and terrible. The men, women, and werewolves were in awe of the great creatures that had been summoned to assist them with the battle. They were huge. Many times larger than what legend had said.

The giant squids, whales, and sharks leapt from the water and devoured entire rows of men on the ships. The squids would land on the ships and throw men down into the water. Their long tentacles wrapped around men, the suckers large enough to rip the face right off a man. They were terrifying.

The kraken lifted entire ships in one great hand and crushed them to powder obliterating the people onboard them. There were great sounds, like a thump, that nobody had heard before occurred each time the kraken crushed ships. The kraken also had fearsomely huge jaws. He devoured entire ships.

The leviathan was terrifying, also devouring entire ships whole, their crews screaming. The Leviathan would jump from the water and land on the ships crushing them into the deep.

Perhaps the most fearsome was the hydra. She breathed fire and vaporized entire ships. The vampires fought her fiercely. She was formidable. They began to sever her heads from their necks. Maug began to fear, he thought all was lost. The stumps began to bubble, and where there was one head missing, two more heads grew in its place. The old tales were true. Cut off one head and two more shall grow in its place. Maug was in awe.

It did not take long. Within minutes the entire fleet was gone. A few floating scraps of wood. Several thousand vampires had seen the sense to abandon their ships. Those that did not make it to the shore were dead in seconds. Then the sea was calm once more. They took their journey past the wrecked fleet of their enemies, and on toward the Great Ocean.

Before they departed, the kraken swam over to their ship. He dropped a large stick with something glinting on the end down onto the deck. Then, he too departed. Red-fang ran forward. It was the javelin that he had launched at the large bat. And the dragon scale was still tied to the end. The kraken had returned his family heirloom to him. He could not have been more happy at that moment. Just then a weeping Maug ran over and embraced him. Maug had no words for him, just a long brotherly embrace.

Although an accident, Red-fang had restored Maug's powers. Things were taking a turn for the better with their expedition.

Chapter Ten
Pursuit

The battle had been incredible and fearsome, and they did not speak much of it. Most of the men and women were in awe of what Maug had accomplished. Summoning those massive sea creatures to help them win past the blockade. The speed with which those fearsome creatures had accomplished the destruction of the enemy fleet was frightening. They continued their journey down the Great River Atlantis.

Their journey down the river became monotonous. Day after day nothing but rowing. They had been traveling for a while when they came to the Rocks of the River. Giant boulders that were in the water. They formed a chain that made sailing to the sea difficult. The chain of rocks was very difficult to navigate. They could only travel during the day.

The manner of travel was very difficult. They had to have a man in the crow's nest using the seeing glass. He would look for rocks and sand bars in their path. When he saw one he would make a signal and they would drop the sea anchor, slowing the ship to a crawl. He would come down and help them to navigate around it. This meant that it could take them a few hours to traverse a mile.

At their center was an island. They decided to visit this island for themselves. The island was rumoured to have hundreds of plant species and deeper in the island it was thought to have wild game that they could hunt. It was also rumoured to be dangerous.

At first Maug was against visiting this island as there were dangerous rumours about this island that had been floating about for years. But he did not know if they were to be believed. In the end he agreed that they could visit the island. This was a mistake. It was here that Yarteb decided to leave. He did not want to help them any more. He missed his family at the palace, and had grown up in fear of this island. So he left.

They arrived on the island. Four men were left on board to maintain the ship. Jayshon, Jayton, Meelite, and Comlick remained on the ship to watch over things. The rest of them took small craft that were stored below deck and traveled to the island.

The island was incredibly beautiful. There were fruits of every color growing everywhere. There were apple trees. There were pear trees. There were peaches, apricots, oranges, lemons, limes, cherries, coconuts, grapefruits, nectarines, mangos, plums, and pomegranates. There were great purple plants that looked like pumpkins; when they were cut open there were bunches of grapes inside. There were hundreds of varieties of food here. They were enjoying themselves greatly.

They built up great bonfires at night and began to share stories with one another. Their stories grew wilder and wilder.

"So, there I was, a young werewolf running through the forest," said Gray-claw. "When suddenly three great bears began chasing me and then..." His words were lost, most people were too drunk to process what he was saying. They were reveling in their victory. They sang songs, and danced dances. There were great games and wrestling matches.

One night the fairy took Maugh to the far side of the island. She told him of her people, how she loved this land so when her people had left she had remained behind. She told him how at first it had not been by choice, she had been banished. She had spent thousands of years alone. She told him of how she had never been loved or been in love, and how she had feared that she would spend her entire life alone. They embraced, and Maug was in ecstasy, that simple hug brought him incredible joy. It was true what they said, fairies gave powerful hugs. Maug stepped back. Tears flowed from his eyes.

"I am deeply in love with you, but this is wrong. In order for things to be right we should be married. We should not engage in physical relations outside of marriage. It is a custom that my father taught me. I always promised myself that I would wait for marriage. That cursed vampire imprisoned all of our priests and we didn't bring any with us. There is no way that we can be married." The fairy looked sad, but she nodded.

"I agree, Maug. We should be married first. It saddens me that we may never be married. But you are right," she said.

A voice spoke to them. "Would you like to be married? I couldn't help overhearing your conversation. I am a priestess to my people. I have performed many marriages."

"Yes!" They both cried in unison. In front of them, a mermaid was treading water a few feet into the river.

"Come into the water, and I will marry you. I will need to know your names." They stepped into the water.

"I am Maug," said Maug. "But I do not know your name my dear," he said, turning to the fairy.

"Oh, right. My name is Taylor," she said with a giggle.

"Very well," said the Mermaid. "By the ancient rites of my people, by the power of the water, and with the blessing of Poseidon, I marry you. Taylor and Maug. I now pronounce you man and wife. You may now kiss." And with this she swam away.

Maug and Taylor caught each other in a fierce embrace. The feeling of her lips on his, the scent of her hair. The feeling of her body in his arms. They spent that night together alone. They were both happy for having waited for marriage before being physically intimate. It made the experience that much sweeter.

When they woke they were both in a happy, peaceful state of mind. The next morning as they were walking back they encountered a cave that they had not before noticed. They went inside, there were scratches on the walls. Suddenly a spirit came out of the wall.

"You must leave this place," said the spirit. "I was trapped here. Time passes more slowly. If you do not leave soon you will be trapped and die here. Every second you spend on this island is an hour in the outside world. This island holds the mysteries of time. You must go." Then he vanished.

"I think we are in trouble," said Maug. They left the cave and ran to the other side of the island. But everyone was gone.

. . .

Erip Mav awoke in his chambers in the palace. His beautiful wife was stroking his face. He tried to sit up, but was unable to move. Something was very wrong.

"What happened?" he asked. He was afraid. He did not think that he could have been defeated so easily. He also could not remember what happened. What was going on? Where were his men? Why was he not at the river? He felt very, very weak. Again he tried to sit up. This time he succeeded but his wife pushed him back down.

"I will be right back," said Taylee, and she left the room. Erip sat there for what felt like hours, though it could only have been minutes. Finally she returned. She had brought with her the vampire shaman. Relaeh, the wisest shaman among vampires who knew the most about healing their kind.

Different blood has different properties. Cow blood is good for ulcers. Horse blood was good for leg injuries. Dog blood was good for the nose. Bird blood was good for the wings. Human blood was obviously the best, as it was good for everything. This much Erip Mav knew. His trusted shaman Relaeh knew about all the bloods.

"My Lord," said Relaeh, with a deep bow. "I am sorry that you have not recovered. It has been some weeks since the battle of the blockade. We were unsure if you would recover at all."

"Not recover at all?!" sputtered Erip Mav. "I am a vampire! I am the lord of the vampires. Why would I not recover?"

"My Lord," said Relaeh. "You were attacked with silver. Somehow, Maug injected a small amount of silver into each of your cells. It has taken all of my skill, and my most powerful magic to help you. You will not be back to full strength for some time my Lord. I am so sorry that I could not do more to help you. I have done what I could. You were lucky that you were not stripped of your power and turned into a mortal. It is beyond my ken how Maug was able to do this to you."

"Injected, all my cells?" Erip Mav was dumbfounded. "Silver?"

"Yes my Lord," said Relaeh.

"My husband, let us not dwell on such madness. Let us rejoice. Let's have a giant feast," said Taylee. "Besides, our son and our people want to see you." She turned to Relaeh, "Will he be well enough to attend a feast by this evening?" She asked.

"I don't see why not," said Relaeh.

"Excellent! I will prepare a feast. Erip, our son will be so excited. He loves the shows the humans put on at the feasts for us!" said Taylee, and she left to prepare the feast.

Erip Mav remained in bed until the feast. His son came to visit. His son had been so worried about him. They embraced. His son was excited to show him how his magical abilities had improved in Erip's absence. He had become very powerful. Erip was very proud of him. He believed his son was nearly ready to be taught the secrets of dark magics. Dark magics reserved only for masters. Soon it was time to head down to the feast.

The feast was glorious and wonderful. The human slaves came and performed a play called "Erip the Great." It was about how Erip Mav had taken over the land. It was artfully performed.

Erip Mav and his friends were greatly amused by this play. It was very enjoyable for all in attendance.

After the feast and the performance Erip Mav retired to his chambers. He was very weary. He was so grateful for his wife. The feast had been excellent. Their play had been great. He had enjoyed it greatly. But he was tired.

The next day he went to see his great friend and ally, Nairotsih. He was a master of history. He was concerned that he had not yet ferreted out all of the secrets of this palace. He needed to know more. To that end he sought out Nairotsih.

"My old friend, I was worried that you would not recover! How are you, my Lord?" said Nairotsih.

"I am well, but I am very angry and frustrated," said Erip Mav. "Our recent defeat was humiliating, but that is not what has me worried the most. Our recent expedition to find the Dragon Scale keys has failed. There was a strange note left in the center of the maze we went to. It said that the keys had been brought to the palace. I know of no such hiding place. You and I searched high and low throughout the entire palace. We've been here for years. I do not know if there is anywhere that we have not yet discovered. Do you?"

"Well, my Lord, there are rumours, and they are only rumours that I read about in another city. Would you like to hear them?" asked Nairotsih. He was very concerned. He had never before put much stock in such rumours and he hoped that his Lord would not either. He would leave that up to his Lord.

"Yes. Of course I do," said Erip. He was annoyed that Nairotsih would even ask such a thing, but he restrained his anger. He knew that Nairotsih was very wise when it came to history.

"Well my Lord. There are rumours throughout the kingdom. Rumours about… Well, my Lord, about a secret chamber hidden here in the castle. It is where you would least expect it sir and I personally find it highly unlikely that it is there," said Nairotsih.

"Well, where is it?" Ask Erip Mav.

"In the library," said Nairotsih.

"In the library? Are you jesting?" Erip Mav roared with laughter. This was the most preposterous thing that he had ever heard. Why would anyone hide anything in a library? This was crazy. "I've heard enough. I am going to go outside to search for the entrance to this secret chamber." Erip Mav got up and began to walk away.

"No, my Lord. I do not jest." Nairotsih had expected this response. He knew Erip Mav would not take this seriously. So he had to explain. "My Lord, please listen to me. My experience and expertise is in history. Let me explain my theory." Erip Mav paused.

"Very well, I will let you explain your theory," said Erip Mav, returning to his seat at the table. He was dubious at best but he was willing to listen to theories at this point. He needed those keys. So he was ready to listen.

"My Lord, too many people do not value history and learning. This is one of the reasons that you have forged a relationship with me, and we are great friends. You love and care for history. It has helped you to become a great conqueror by understanding the history of your enemies," said Nairotsih. "If you were going to hide something wouldn't you do it in a place of learning and history? A place where most men would not go?" As Nairotsih finished he saw a glint in Erip Mav's eyes, a glint he had seen there many times before.

"I understand what you are saying," said Erip Mav. "Hide it in plain sight!"

"Yes, indeed my Lord," said Nairotsih.

"I agree. Hiding them in plain sight would be an excellent idea. I will search through this library here in the palace," said Erip Mav. He stood up and walked away.

Erip Mav walked to the library and opened the doors. The library was beautiful. He had truly never seen anything like it. There were hundreds of rows of books. There were ladders next to each row so that one could access the upper shelves. The shelves were marked according to their subjects. These occupied the walls to his right and his left. In front of him there was an empty space, hundreds of square feet. There were tables here for reading, and studying. Between the tables and the shelves were dark shapes.

He was staring at statues, thousands of them. There were statues of the gods and goddesses all over the library. They showed them sitting on thrones, fighting fearsome beasts, and forging terrifying weapons. There were also statues of the kings and queens. In an earlier age there had been dragons in the land. Here they were depicted in stone. The statues of the dragons were the most life-like. They depicted battles, and fearsome they were. He saw elves and fairies depicted here. Some of the fairies were bigger than he. He saw many were-kind depicted mid-transformation. There were also wolves, tigers, bears, lions, and hundreds of other animals depicted here. There were depicted dwarves forging weapons and mining gemstones. The statues were glorious and wonderful. Truly they were a sight to behold.

He was amazed at what the humans had accomplished. He began to reconsider his actions towards them. His hatred for humans ran deep. So deep that it seemed to flow within his veins.

Hatred for being suppressed. Hatred for being banished to the wastelands far to the north. Hatred for what humans stood for. And yet here he stood in this beautiful library looking at the works of humans. He even took the time to read some of their books. Were humans at fault for all the atrocities that took place in this world? Were humans truly to be despised for hating dark creatures? Should humans be punished for the actions of their ancestors and of Pathorian the Wise? No, not necessarily. Humans were not to blame. Did this mean that he should stop? Should demons really be released? Yes! Demons did not deserve the oppression that they had received. He would release them. Should he stop his mission and reevaluate his choices? No, he would not be dissuaded from his mission. He slammed closed the book he was examining and continued his search.

He wandered around in the library for hours tapping on the statues seeing if there was a passage in one of them. He pulled random books off shelves to see if they activated trap doors. No such luck. He ordered his food to be brought to the library so that he could eat while he worked. Raw steak, soaked in blood, with blood pudding and blood whiskey. This was one of his favorite meals.

He searched for hours and hours. Then, he remembered what Nairotsih had said "If you were going to hide something wouldn't you do it in a place of learning and history? A place where most men would not go." He also remembered how this statement had caused him to think about hiding things in plain sight. It was so simple. Why had he not started there? He walked to the center of the room and found a giant dragon statue.

. . .

They ran around the island calling everyone's names. Soon they found them playing and dancing near another cave. They could hear the festivities from several hundred yards away. There were five great bonfires.

Over two bonfires they were roasting great pigw. Over another fire they were roasting a very large turkey. Over a fourth fire they were roasting a massive deer. Around the fire in the middle there were a great many of the crew singing and dancing. They were chanting. "We can live forever here. We can live forever here. We do not need to leave. We do not need to leave. If we stay we will be happy. If we stay we will be happy. This place is eternal. This place is eternal. Rah rah rah. Rah rah rah." They were repeating this chant over and over again with a ritualistic dance to go with it. Maug doused their fire with magic and interrupted the revelry.

"Why are you doing this? Have you forgotten about our oath? We must find the rightful prince. What are you people doing?" said Maug.

"What are you doing?!" screamed Christian. "We were enjoying ourselves!"

"You have no right to interrupt our fun!" said one man.

"I agree!" said another man.

"Let's throw them in the ocean!" scream a third man.

"No! Stop! We should listen," said a fourth man.

"You're an idiot!" said a fifth man to the fourth man who spoke.

"Let's kill them!" yelled a sixth man, and he leapt forward. Maug threw up a magical shield, the man was thrown back. The fairy gasped but otherwise did not react. She remained stoic throughout the exchange. Fairies were a hardy and powerful people. It took a lot to phase them.

"Stop all of you!" cried Maug. "You are under the influence of the plants here. They are warping your minds. You must listen!" Maug augmented his next statement with a healing spell to hopefully help them snap out of it. "You must all stop. What are you doing? I demand that you be healed." They all seemed to come too at once.

"Maug, what is going on?" asked Christian.

"Christian, Red-fang, my friends there is something in these plants that affects us. Like a drug," said Maug. "Who here has eaten of the grapes that live within the purple pumpkin like plants?" Everyone raised their hands except for Maug and the fairy, Taylor. They made their way back to the ship. They made their preparations to leave. They believed that it would be safe to take the meat that they had collected with them as none of the animals could break open the purple pumpkins.

. . .

This large dragon statue in the center of the room was very impressive to Erip Mav. He approached it, he noticed an inscription upon it. *Take care that ye be pure of heart before you enter. Prove your worth to enter the room where the prophecies are kept. If you are worthy you may enter. If you pass the test you are allowed to take the item that you declare. If you are not worthy, then you will die within the room. Follow the instructions of the guardian Dragon to escape unscathed*

"Lord Mav," said Leecher. Erip Mav turned away from the statue.

"Yes Leecher?"

"We must depart immediately. Now that you are strong again we should pursue the rebels. I have prepared a group of sprinter class vessels. Use the seeing stone and you will be able to find them and lead us to them," said Leecher. Erip Mav thought for a moment. Leecher was absolutely right. They needed to pursue the rebels. He would worry about this guardian dragon later.

"Very well, Leecher. Let us go to this fleet of vessels. You are correct. The rebels must be stopped," said Erip Mav. On the way Leecher explained how he had only been able to prepare ten sprinter class vessels. Erip Mav only hoped that it would be enough.

Because the king was still weak they needed to travel the old fashioned way to Port City. They rode horses. The same black, red eyed horses that pulled their carriages coming into the kingdom all those years ago.

It took them about a week of traveling but they finally reached Port City. They boarded the sprinter class vessels and began their journey. Using the seeing stone Erip Mav was able to determine that the rebels were on an island. His people called this island "Timeless Isle". Time flows differently on this island.

"Leecher, why do you think the rebels would go to Timeless Isle? Surely they know that it is extremely dangerous. Surely they know that there is a purple pumpkin there that houses hallucinogenic grapes. Grapes that cause you to become so addicted that you can never leave the island again. Surely they know this. Don't you think?" said Erip Mav.

"My Lord, I do not know. Maybe they do not know all of the stories. Maybe they know nothing at all. After all, they are only tiny weak humans," said Leecher. They approached the island. They got closer and closer. Then they saw the Purple Dragon. They began to surround the ship.

. . .

When Maug and his people arrived back at the ship they were greatly disturbed. Jayshon, Jayton, Meelite, and Comlick were in a panic. There were vessels approaching them from all sides. They were going to be surrounded within minutes. There would be no escape. Maug began chanting. He summoned up great fog to mask their ship and confuse their enemies. Under the cover of this fog they escaped. They did a head count when they arrived back at the ship. Only to discover that Yarteb was no longer with them. Christian and Maug conducted interviews. It turned out the Yarteb had never come to the island with them. Where could he be?

They search high and low for Yarteb. They could not find him anywhere on the ship. They even searched for him using magic. He was not on the ship. This was not good.

Chapter Eleven
Betrayal

Erip Mav was furious. The rebels had slipped through his clutches again. But there was some good news. They had a prisoner. Yarteb was his name. Although Erip Mav was not sure that prisoner was the correct word to describe him.

Yarteb had been caught skulking around one of the steam bridges near the end of the River Atlantis. He claimed that he had left the rebels; he said that he disagreed with them. He now wanted them caught. It was thanks to him that they had found the rebels and nearly caught them a second time.

He told Erip Mav of their plans to travel to the east and find the merfolk and the fairies. They eventually planned to find the prince. Erip Mav was very intrigued by this.

"How did they discover the whereabouts of the prince?" Ask Erip Mav.

"It was written in something called "The third volume of the book of knowledge". Or something like that. I do not remember what it was called," said Yarteb. He couldn't remember the name of the book but he did remember the prophecy. He thought that this might be important. "My Lord, I do remember the prophecy," said Yarteb.

"Oh, you do? Tell it to me, now," said Erip Mav. Erip Mav hope that Yarteb was not lying. He needed to know the prophecy. "Did it come from the third volume of the book of prophecy perhaps?"

"Yes it did," said Yarteb. He continued. "I got the sense that they didn't tell me everything. But I will tell you what I remember. '*There will come a day of darkness. A day when vampires and other bloodthirsty creatures infest the land. The vampire leader will call himself Erip Mav. He is an ancient vampire. He is very powerful and he is thousands of years old. We have seen the boy who can defeat him. Before we tell you about the boy you must know about the plans of the vampire. He has been communicating through a seeing stone with some demons in the netherworld. He has agreed to release these demons if they help*

him to conquer our world and other worlds.

Please know that it is not just our world at stake. There are

thousands of worlds at stake. It is down to you who are reading

this prophecy to help save them. Trillions of innocent and free

souls are counting on you. You must not fail them. Fear not, we

will give you all the tools that you need to succeed.

Prophecy is not an exact art. The future is in flux, the

movement of one grain of sand here on this world can affect the

lives of billions of people elsewhere. So conversely can the lives of

billions of people elsewhere affect a grain of sand here on this

world. Even those of us who can peer through time do not always

understand what we see. We simply record it, and hope that our

scarier prophecies will not come to pass. In the event that they do,

we attempt to impart to you in the future the tools you need to save

the worlds.

If you do not embark on this journey, great evil will hold

this land for millions of years to come. Trillions of people throughout the known worlds will be enslaved. If you fail, it will

mean failure for all worlds. Dark vapor will cover the lands,

children will be stripped from their mothers to either become food

for demons, or transformed into lesser demons. Vampires will have

free reign. There will be great horror. The stuff of nightmares will

be an everyday reality for most people. Those who are not killed

will live as slaves to service the every whim of the demons. Death,

destruction, darkness, these will be the reality. Creatures of light

will all be killed or banished. Those who are not killed or banished

will be corrupted into hideous shadows of their true selves. Fear,

fear will be a daily feeling for people. Light will never abide in the

known worlds again. If you do not embark on your journey, you

will condemn thousands of worlds to darkness, destruction, and

death. Darkness will reign, and when it does no one will find

peace.

We know that this is a scary prospect. We long debated

whether or not to record this prophecy for the fear that it would

cause. We were concerned that if we recorded this prophecy that it would become self fulfilling. We were afraid that we would lead

you to inaction, and your inaction would lead to the darkness that

we have foreseen.

The gift of foresight is not perfect. As we have said, the

future is in flux. We give you this one hope: within everyone is the

ability to naturally dispel darkness from within. You must embark;

we are forbidden to write about who you should take with you. We

remind you that the future is very much in flux. Anything can

happen. We foresee great things from all of you.

Also, we have seen the futures. We do not know which

future will come to pass. We cannot stress enough to you that the

future is in flux. The future shifts, and changes. You must be aware

of this. You must know that our prophecies could be vastly wrong.

But we are wise. In a sense we have traveled millions of years, in

millions of years of seeing the future and recording our prophecies

we have never seen, or in other words "met" someone who is not

of value. Remember that you are unique. You are all unique and

special. You can be successful. Do not fear the future, only believe in yourself. Good luck in your journeys. May the light and hope be with you always. May you vanquish all of your foes.' This is what I remember of the prophecy," said Yarteb. "Have I gained your trust? Can I be on your side?"

"We will see," said Erip Mav. "You have done me a great service today. I look forward to our next conversation." Erip Mav snapped his fingers and some burly vampires escorted Yarteb from the room. Erip Mav had another thing that he needed to tackle. Another problem, that of the dragon. In order to tackle this, he wanted to speak to his wife.

Erip Mav returned to his chambers after a day of thinking and pondering what to do. He finally decided it could not wait any longer. He needed to speak with Taylee. She was reading spells of dark magic off of his personal scrolls by candle light. "My beloved, I have some questions for you," said Erip Mav

"Yes love? What is it?" said Taylee.

"Have you heard of the room of prophecy, and the book of prophecy?' inquired Erip Mav.

"Yes I have. Why do you want to know about them?" Taylee put down the scrolls and was now stared intently at her husband. Erip Mav cleared his throat.

"Do you remember when I went on that expedition to the north?" he asked.

"Yes," she said. "I was terribly worried about you. I did not know if you would return. You were gone for so long. What about it?"

"We went there searching for the dragon scale keys. To help us open up portals to the netherworld. Our search led us to the caves of Margeth. We followed the maze to the center of the caves. The keys weren't there. They had already been taken," said Erip Mav. He was greatly concerned that she would not be able to help him. "And there was a note. The note stated that the keys would be taken to the hall of prophecy. Do you know where it is?" Taylee sighed and shook her head.

"Unfortunately I do not know where it is," she said. "It may or may not be hidden under the great dragon in the library. I have always thought that it was hidden there, but I never tried to enter."

. . .

Maug and his crew had traveled to the edge of Orcalias, their home country. They were currently anchored at a port city. This city was a flourishing center of trade. This city, the city Michael sat on the edge of the sea and the River Atlantis. It was one of the greatest cities on this side of The Shoulders, a mountain range spanning north to south separating the coast from the rest of the mainland. They did not know what lay beyond. They felt that they should rest here for a time before continuing on. So that is what they did. They should not have done so.

They enjoyed their time. Lavishing their money on the beauty of the city. There was a great theatre in this town. They performed great songs and told great stories. There was an old man who told a great story about being out on the open sea and encountering the isle of the singers.

"When I was a young lad I encountered something very strange. I was far out to sea. Farther than anyone had been before. If you'll believe it we were out on the open sea. We encountered an island," said the old man. He seemed to repeat details as he was very drunk. "As we approached the island we heard beautiful singing. So we went to this island." The old man continued his story, occasionally hiccuping due to his consumption of so much alcohol. "On the island there were gorgeous women. They sang beautiful songs to us. We were entranced and intoxicated. Then, they stopped singing. We longed to hear that wonderful music again. We begged them and begged them to sing. I decided that it was not worth it and returned to the ship. I waited and waited. But they did not return. Then one day many old men came to the ship from the island. I did not recognize them. As it turns out they were my crew. The women on the island had stolen their youth and vitality. Making them old beyond measure. By the time we arrived back here they were all dead. There were many investigations. They even sent an expedition to the island that did not return. I have lived out my life as a lonely man. I own the ship, but nobody will sail with me. So I sail myself. I have been alone all these years. Thank you for listening to my sad sorry tale. I bid you adieu." With that the old man bowed, banging his head into the ground, and left. Gray-claw turned to Maug.

"Do you think he was telling the truth?" said Gray-claw. He was very intrigued by the possibility that there really was such an island.

"I do not know. There are many strange things in our world," said Maug.

"I don't know, I think that old geezer is crazy," said Red-fang. He had scoffed through the whole performance. He was a skeptic when it came to many tales. He did not believe things easily. He set his basis in facts.

"I could stay here forever!" Christian said to Maug.

"Ah, I agree. But we cannot stay here forever," said Maug. "We must depart soon."

"Why must we depart? I do not understand. I know that we are on an important mission. But can we not stay for a time here?" asked Christian.

"I suppose I can delay our departure for a few more days. But we must leave soon," said Maug.

"Thank you," said Christian.

"There is a time and place for everything. Perhaps we can return here when our journey is over and the worlds are saved," said Maug. He agreed that this place was beautiful. He would have loved to stay here. He found it wonderful and beautiful. The artists here were wonderful as well.

"I think that we need to be careful not to get sucked into anything strongly," said Taylor the fairy. "We have a mission to perform."

"You are right of course," said Christian.

"Thank you," said the fairy. She saw a great maturity in him.

"We should head back to the ship for the night. I do not think that we should leave the ship alone for any length of time," said Maug. They all agreed with him so they returned to the ship. There were dwarves trying to leave with their ship!

. . .

Erip Mav had gone to the library. He had read many books about the library and what was going on with the library. After a few hours of searching he was drawn to the great statue in the center of the room. He walked to the center of the room and read the inscription on the chest of the dragon again.

Take care that ye be pure of heart before you enter. Prove your worth to enter the room where the prophecies are kept. If you are worthy you may enter. If you pass the test you are allowed to take the item that you declare. If you are not worthy, then you will die within the room. Follow the instructions of the guardian Dragon to escape unscathed

"Are you the guardian dragon?" asked Erip Mav. There was a great roar as the statue reared its head.

"Hello vampire. I am the guardian dragon, what do you seek?" said the statue. Erip Mav marveled. He was slightly dumbstruck. He didn't know how to react to the dragon before him. It was made of stone; in the olden days he had witnessed entire legions of vampires devoured by single dragons. He did not know what to say. Was there a password, or a keyphrase? Something that he was supposed to say? He did not know. He sat there pondering what to say. He sat there for so long that the dragon began to laugh. "You don't know what is needed do you?"

"I wish to find the dragon scale keys that can open portals," said Erip Mav. The dragon roared with laughter.

"You vampire. Why do you seek the keys?" asked the dragon. This gave Erip Mav some pause. What should he say? Did this dragon know his true intent? How did the dragon know that he sought the keys? He was so confused. He was unsure. How could he trust the stone creature? He did not know what to say. So he decided on the truth.

"Well, I feel that demon-kind needs to be released and freed," said Erip Mav

"Please continue," said the dragon statue.

"Well, demon-kind has been suppressed for centuries. Millennia actually. I think that they should be released. I would use the dragon scale keys to release demon-kind. When that is done, I would conquer the other worlds," said Erip Mav.

"Well, my young vampire. I do not know what to do with you. You are a strange individual. You want to unleash such evil, but yet you are pure in heart. What an enigma," said the dragon statue.

"If I am pure of heart, may I enter?" said Erip Mav.

"Give me time to think," said the dragon statue. The statue pondered for a long time on what to do. This vampire was an enigma. Vampires were inherently evil, and yet this vampire is pure in heart.

"Well, may I enter?" said Erip Mav. Erip Mav did not know what it meant to be pure in heart. He thought he understood. It meant he had a good heart. But he, like all vampires, was evil.

"Silence," said the dragon. "I must consider you further." The dragon thought about what his creator had told him. He could always trust the pure in heart no matter what was on the outside.

. . .

Maug and his people ran to the ship and began to fight the dwarves. These dwarves were sick with the gold fever and were attempting to separate the celestial iron from the ship. They were not able to, as it was one seamless piece of celestial iron that had been magicked in place.

"What are you doing!?" shouted Maug.

"We want this vessel for ourselves. We will claim this celestial iron," shouted the dwarven leader.

"NO!" said Taylor the fairy. She raised her hands and attempted to throw the dwarves off the ship. They had their own spell caster. As Taylor was still very weak she could not counter him. He blocked her spell. Then he threw her into the ocean, he used his magic to push her down into the water. He pushed her so far that she began to sink. Maug dove off the ship after her. He had to swim down dozens of feet.

When he finally reached her she was tangled in some parasitic weeds. They flowed around her as if through air. He had to cut and hack at them for at least a dozen seconds. He was beginning to lose air. He did not know how long fairies could remain underwater. He was not optimistic. He fought the weeds and fought them. It was then, when he had given up all hope that help came.

The mermaid who had married him and Taylor appeared. In short order she bit all of the plants and they retreated back into the sand. The mermaid left. They swam back up to the surface.

In the time that they had been underwater Christian and the other were-wolves had captured the leader of the dwarves and his captains. There were ten of these captains.

"I demand you let us go!" screamed the dwarven leader.

"Oh, don't worry. We will," said Maug.

"When?" demanded the dwarven leader.

"Why, now of course." Maug said. He gave a forceful nod and the dwarves were all thrown overboard.

"Ho to! Weigh anchors! Men and women down to the oars. It is time to leave!" shouted Maug. With that they were off. They left the port city of Michael and were on their way to the west.

. . .

"Well, my little vampire. You are certainly an enigma," said the dragon. "Because you are pure in heart I will let you pass. But you must be cautious."

"Thank you," said Erip Mav. The dragon lifted his paws, opened a trap door. "Enter," said the dragon.

Erip Mav entered the room of prophecy. There were powerful things here. Things so powerful that they could not be spoken of. A ring of keys in a case with the inscription *These keys can open up portals anywhere, including the netherworld. Use them wisely.* There were potions to kill with a single drop. There were books about magic and all kinds of other philosophies. There was a shelf that said "The Book of Prophecy".

He ignored it all and went straight for the keys. He took the keys and left the room. He did not take the keys to his room; he had decided to keep them on his person. He did not want them to be stolen or misused by anyone. Erip Mav returned to the throne room with the keys hidden on his person. He pondered his newly found good fortune. He had the keys. Now, he had to find out how they worked. In the meantime he wanted to interrogate Yarteb. He had Yarteb brought to the throne room.

"So Yarteb, tell me all you know. I am trying to decide what to do with you," said Erip Mav. "I could keep you as a human slave. I could turn you into a vampire. I could banish you for betraying your friends. I do not know what I should do with you. So tell me what you want and why I should grant it to you."

"I know a lot about your enemies," said Yarteb.

"What do you know about my enemies?" said Erip Mav. He was intrigued by this man more and more with each interview.

He was unsure how to proceed. He had some ideas; however he was interested in what Yarteb wanted. "Well, speak, Yarteb. The time is yours to defend yourself and tell me what you want."

"I know that there are now one hundred and one people with Maug on that ship," said Yarteb. "I further know that there is a fairy traveling with them, and she is the one who outfitted their ship. She is very powerful. I further know that they intend to travel to the east. I believe that is where the former king's great-grandson is. I also know that they have been in contact with your sworn enemy, the were-king White-tail. He is the one who helped rally your enemies to your cause. Including myself. I crave your forgiveness for joining with your enemies, my Lord. I wish to become a vampire. I would join your ranks in pursuit of your enemies."

"Tell me, you betrayed your friends. How do I know that you will not betray me too?" said Erip Mav.

"To put it frankly, my Lord, I agree with your agenda. I would see the demons released from their prison," said Yarteb. "I support your desire to liberate all imprisoned creatures, including demons."

"Oh, and why else should I grant this to you?" said Erip Mav.

"My Lord, I wish only to serve you. I wish to atone for my transgression. I want to help join you in your noble quest," said Yarteb.

"Very well. I will give you quarters here in the palace. I will not turn you into a vampire just yet. You must give me time to make that decision," said Erip Mav.

"Thank you, my Lord," said Yarteb, with a deep bow.

"Of course, human. Guards, escort him to chambers in the west wing," said Erip Mav. Then Erip left the palace. He wandered around the town reveling in how he inspired fear in the presence of his subjects. His human slaves. He was greatly joyed by what he had accomplished. Soon his son came out to join him. They walked together in the streets. Then his son asked him a disturbing question.

"Father, why are we trying to free the demons? Won't they hurt us?" asked his son.

"Why do you ask me this, my son?" said Erip Mav.

"I am worried, father. I do not want to let the demons out. I am afraid of them. I also want to find my half brother."

"What do you mean?" said Erip Mav. He was greatly disturbed by what his son had said. "My son, why would you be afraid? Who told you that you had a half brother?"

"The humans I study with are afraid of demons. My tutor is also afraid of demons. From all the stories, demons are horrible. Mother told me about her other son. By logic he is my half brother. You never told me that I had a half brother. Why did you never tell me about him?"

"Well my son, that is a long story. Before I came to this land your mother loved another man. He was killed when I took over the land. Before I took over, your mother feared me. She sent your half brother away. I am searching for him so that we can be a proper family," said Erip Mav. "She was distraught when we met and I wanted to give her the gift of immortality, so I turned her into a vampire. Eventually we fell in love. Then we had you. I have had your mother taught in the dark magics to become as powerful as I am. Now, onto your questions about the demons. In exchange for being released, the demons will serve me. You will have nothing to fear from them. Do you understand?"

"Are you sure, Father? Why must we release the demons anyway? They were locked up for a reason, weren't they? Well, they must have been very powerful to have needed to be locked up like that. So why release them?" his son asked.

"Those are excellent questions, my son. I just feel like I should release them. I promise that if I do everything will be well," said Erip Mav.

"I trust you, Father," said his son. They returned to the palace and Erip Mav took his son to their chambers. Then he went to the throne room and summoned his son's teacher to come before him. His son's teacher was human; perhaps that had been a mistake.

"Why have you told my son that you fear demons? Would you turn my own son against me?!" Erip shouted the last word. His son's teacher, Mary by name, quivered before Erip Mav.

"My Lord, I crave your pardon. I didn't mean to turn him against you. I would never do such a thing," said Mary. "I only wanted the boy to be aware of how us humans feel. Isn't that why you chose a human teacher for your son? So that we could instruct him in these other perspectives."

"You will stop this now. You will only teach my son what I approve and authorize." Erip Mav stated in an icy cold voice. Erip stood and produced an iron rod from his robes. "Kneel before me!" bellowed Erip Mav.

"No! Please, My Lord, I beg you. I meant no harm. Please, NO!" The woman screamed. Erip Mav smiled.

"You must be punished so that you will not make the same mistake again," said Erip Mav. He snapped his fingers and chains bound her in place. He began to chant. Soon the end of the iron rod grew cherry red. Erip Mav continued to chant, then it was glowing white hot.

"No, my Lord." whispered Mary. "Please do not mark me."

"You must be marked." whispered Erip Mav. Then he touched her with the iron.

"AHHHH!" Screamed Mary. She was left with a circle burned into her chest, just below the neck. He had the guards pull her to her feet. Then he had her dragged from the hall. He was still furious. He had Leecher and Lightning summoned to the throne room. He needed to tell them about his discovery.

"I found the secret chamber in the library and I found the Dragon Scale keys. The problem is that I have no idea how to use them at all," said Erip Mav.

"How would you learn how to use them?" asked Lightning

"the demons might know how. Mightn't they?" said Leecher.

"Yes, and Erip Mav can talk to them through his seeing stones. At least that is what you've told us, Erip," said Lightning.

"I can communicate with them. But to a very limited degree. Mostly just to tell them what I am doing. They cannot always communicate back," said Erip Mav.

"Well that's useless. But no matter, could we not go and commune with the jinn again? I'm sure that he would be able to tell us how to use the keys," said Leecher.

"I do not know how I feel about that," said Lightning.

"Then what are we going to do?" asked Erip Mav

"What do you mean?" asked Leecher.

"We have to do something to find out how the keys work," said Erip Mav.

"Why don't we try trial and error?" asked Lightning.

"Hmm, very well," said Erip Mav. "Let's try it your way. I hope for your sake that we succeed quickly."

Chapter Twelve
A Narrow Escape

The dwarves hadn't done any significant damage to their ship. However, they would have to be more careful in the future. They couldn't leave the ship alone again. Not that it would matter for some time: they far out at sea, near a great whirlpool.

"Well," said Christian "The ocean is beautiful." He enjoyed staring at the sea. The rise and fall of the waves was powerful to him. It gave him pride that they were on their journey to find Carlos.

"I agree," said Red-fang. He had mixed feelings about this journey. He was sworn in service to White-tail, and White-tail had demanded that he protect Christian. So that is what he would do. He had some reservations about leaving Orcalias. Orcalias was his home. He did not know why he was afraid to leave. But he was. Fear was a very real thing. Fear was something that he had fought his entire life.

"I too agree," said Gray-claw. He loved the water. They were traveling far away from his home, but he was fine with that. He would protect Christian. That was his job now. So that was what he would do.

"The ocean is also something to be respected and feared," said Maug. "Do not forget the fearsome creatures that we summoned to help us."

"That is true," said Christian. *I'm not likely to forget those in a hurry*, he thought to himself.

"I think that respect is the better word for it," said Gray-claw.

"Perhaps you are right," said Maug.

The four of them sat admiring the water and the dazzling ship for a time. Then they left the deck and went about their duties. They had to scrub the deck, trim the sails. They shimmied their way across the great sail supports and repaired any damage to the sails. This was a difficult and dangerous process. They were all hardened men and women and they worked regardless of the danger.

"Ho!" cried the man in the crow's nest. "There is something off the starboard bow!" Everyone ran to the starboard side of the ship. They did not like what they saw. There was a great funnel of clouds. This was not an ordinary funnel. This funnel was moving sideways towards the ship.

"Ho! Down to the oars!" yelled Maug. "Double time, double time. Full away. Turn us about and get us away from that funnel!" The men and women scrambled to get down belowdeck to the oars. They beat a great drum, and the shouting of Otek their chanter set the tempo. They turned the ship and began to row away from the funnel.

The funnel moved quickly, as though it had a mind of its own. It came closer and closer to them. They could not win free of it. Inch by inch the dragon's tail was slowly enveloped in this cloud. Then with a whooshing sound the entire ship was engulfed in the cloud. Everything went black. It was so black that they could not even light their candles to see.

The only source of light was Maug's glowing staff. The others on the ship begged Maug to tell them a story for they had grown both feared and bored while isolated in this cloud. So Maug told them a story.

"One night, under the starry sky, while out hunting I got separated from my father. I became lost in the forest. It wasn't long before I realized just how alone I was. I wandered around killing rabbits and other small game to stay alive. I began to fear that I would never find my father again. Until one day I found a great black dog wandering around in the forest. He stayed with me. He kept me company for a long time. The days turned into weeks. Until one day my father found me and took me home. I have not seen that dog since then," said Maug.

"Great story!" exclaimed several voices in unison. Maug bowed. Then he and his wife returned to their quarters. Maug had to come back out to escort the rest of the people to their beds as it was still very dark.

That night many of the crew had nightmares about being swallowed up by the ocean. They also dreamed about the cloud that surrounded them. *They dreamed that it flowed into their mouths and took over their bodies. The cloud had intelligence. It took them over and controlled their ship. It forced them to sail far to the south. To the deepest waters. Then the cloud left their bodies. They were far to the south and did not know how they got there. They were so confused.*

. . .

Erip Mav stood in the throne room with Lightning and Leecher. He had shown them the keys and they were trying to make them work. "What if we put them into an actual door?" asked Lightning. "What if it needs to interact with a real door to work?" The other two pondered this for several minutes. They were not sure what Lightning meant.

"What do you mean?" they both asked in unison. They were greatly confused by this notion of putting the keys into real doors.

"Well, think of it like this," said Lightning. He explained that he thought that they needed a real door to interact with because a portal was a door. Now they understood what he meant.

"Well, I suppose you can try it," said Erip Mav. He offered the keys to Lightning. Lightning walked over to the nearest door and put the red key into the lock and turned it. Nothing happened. He tried all of the other keys and nothing happened. He walked back over to Erip Mav and handed him back the keys.

"I am all out of ideas," said Lightning.

"Well there is the Great Library," said Leecher.

"What do you mean?" inquired Lightning.

"The Great Library, where you found the Keys. It has books on all subjects doesn't it?" said Leecher. Erip Mav and Lightning nodded. "Well then, perhaps there is a book there that can instruct us on how to use the Keys."

"An excellent idea," said Erip Mav. "Let us go to the library." So they went to the library and began searching. They were there for hours. Pouring over books, some of them very old. They were having no luck so they left the library to clear their heads. Erip Mav went down to the dungeons.

He inspected the dungeons. All of his prisoners were here. The important prisoners had been transformed into lesser creatures so that they would not cause problems. It had been simple enough to turn them into slugs and such. In fact he had enjoyed doing it. It meant that they could not rebel and cause him problems. As he inspected the dungeons his wife came running up to him. "My beloved," she said.

"What are you doing down here my love?" asked Erip Mav.

"Leecher and Lightning suspected that I would find you here. I am worried about you. Come, let us go on a walk outside the palace," said Taylee.

"Very well, my love, we shall," said Erip Mav. They left the palace and walked outside. They spent several hours together enjoying each other's company. They walked up and down the streets. Sampling the food from the merchants. Breads, cheeses, wine, fish, fowl, and many other things besides. "My love, I am worried," said Erip Mav.

"Why are you worried, my love?" said Taylee.

"Do you think that I am doing the right thing by trying to free demon-kind?" asked Erip Mav. He was unsure how else to voice his concern other than to just voice it. So that is what he did.

"Why on earth would you think that you are doing the wrong thing?" asked Taylee.

"Our son is worried about the demons. And I had a … communication," said Erip Mav.

"What do you mean, you had a communication?" said Taylee.

"I do not know what it was. Someone or something spoke to me. Also I have been having self doubts about the mission I have chosen for myself. Is it the right mission?" said Erip Mav.

"My husband, why would it be the wrong mission?" asked Taylee.

"I am having second thoughts," said Erip Mav. "First our son expresses concerns to me, then the Guardian Dragon allows me to enter the room of prophecies. The Guardian Dragon told me that I was pure in heart. What does that even mean? How can a vampire like me be pure in heart? It doesn't make sense. Do you know what he could have meant?" said Erip Mav. His wife was silent for so long that he thought that she was not going to answer. When she did answer he was very astounded by her response.

"My husband, I fell in love with you because I too believe you to be pure in heart. Things will not always be as they are now. Someday I believe we will no longer be vampires. I have expressed this to our son, this is why he fears the demons. He believes as do I that we will not always be as we are. As for you my husband, I believe that you have a great destiny in shaping the Orcalias to be. I think that you and I have a great destiny together. As does my son Carlos. We all have a great destiny to fulfill, together. Do not fear what you do not understand. There is no such thing as the unknown, only that which we cannot currently see. Someday all shall be revealed, then everything will be known," said Taylee.

Erip Mav nodded. He embraced his wife. They made their way back to the castle together. He needed to go back to the library, he had promised to me Leecher and Lightning there. First he went to see his son.

"Father, come see my progress!" said his son excitedly. He showed his father a giant purple slug with a burn on its neck. Erip Mav roared with laughter.

"Did you transform your teacher into a slug?" asked Erip Mav. He was still smiling. This boy was truly his son.

"Yes father," said the boy. "Are you angry?" he asked.

"No I am not!" said Erip Mav. "Just make sure you turn her back by the end of the day."

"Very well, father," said his son.

Erip Mav went to the library. He met up with Lightning and Leecher. They continued to search the library for the elusive books that they would need. They did not know where the books were that they needed. Erip Mav and Leecher were in different corners of the library when they heard Lightning exclaim, "I think I found it!"

"What do you mean?" said Erip Mav.

"This book here, it talks about teleporting, and portals," said Lightning. "Here, read it for yourselves."

Of all the magics in our world teleportation and portals are the most dangerous. You can teleport anywhere in our world if you can see it, you have been there before, or if it is on a map that you can see. Teleportation is a difficult magic to learn. If you have already learned it I applaud you. You must be powerful.

Now about portals. There are natural portals in Orcalias and the surrounding lands. The ones in Orcalias are protected by potent dragon magic from an age gone by. There are portals in surrounding lands. Far to the east there is a lake that will teleport you to another world. This world is called Earth by its people. Some of our people have traveled there. This planet is beautiful and wondrous. This planet is where great and powerful beings dwell. Our ancestors called them gods. Whether or not they are gods we leave it up to you to decide. If you seek the magics of the portals you must travel to this lake. There is also another place. There is a Hall of Portals. It is watched over by powerful creatures. It is located on earth. It is guarded by those creatures that our ancestors called gods.

There is, of course, another option for creating and using portals. The Dragon Scale Keys. These can create portals anywhere including the nether-world where the demons are kept. You must find the dragon scale keys in order to master portal craft. Once you have the keys you will....

"Where are the missing pages? And where is the rest of this page?" Ask Erip Mav.

"I don't know!" said Lightning. "But it must be here somewhere. It must be right?"

"I do not know," said Leecher.

"Let us search," said Erip Mav. "Where did you find this book?" So Lightning led them to the shelf where he had located the book he now held. They scoured the shelf. They pulled out and looked at volumes that looked promising. But they found nothing. Then Leecher crowed.

"I have found the missing part of that page!" He shouted. "Here read this half page."

need to know how to use them. We can give you some advice here. You must command the keys as if you mean it. Close your eyes and imagine that you are unlocking a door. Push the Dragon Scale key that you are using into the invisible lock and turn it. Then you will be able to open a portal. The key that you use will determine the portal that you open. The red key will open a portal to a world with a red star in its sky. The orange key will open a portal to a volcanic world with rivers of liquid stone; this world has three stars in its sky. The yellow key can open a portal to this world. It will be of little use to you. The green key will open a portal to Earth. The blue key will open a key to a watery world full of merfolk. The indigo key will take you to a world with a blue star in its sky. It is a world of what you will consider twilight. The violet key will open a portal to a world with a dead star in its sky. A world of true night. These are the seven main worlds. There are hundreds of worlds. You can travel to a few of the other worlds using a combination of keys. It is not written in this book how to open a portal to the nether-world. Those secrets are contained in another book.

"At least we have some clues now," said Erip Mav.

"Yes, what do you think of these gods that the book mentions?" said Leecher.

"I do not know what to think. I am very old," said Erip. "There are stories that my father told me about beings, creatures, people, he did not know what to call them. These people were very powerful. They could live for millions of years beyond what vampires live. They were said to be truly immortal. A vampire will wither away given enough time. However, these beings were said never to lose their brilliance. I do not know about them. I do know that we do not have any hope of defeating the gods without the assistance of the demons."

"I agree with you My Lord," said Lightning. "Could we not go ask the Jinn for help? Or travel to the east? We were banished very far to the north, but to the east I have heard that unicorns still bestride the land. Wouldn't they know the secrets of the portals?"

"I do not know," said Leecher. "I say that we continue to search the library for the answers that we seek."

"I agree with Leecher," said Erip Mav. "We will continue to search the library." Erip Mav waited until Leecher and Lightning had departed. Then he approached the dragon statue. "I need your help again," he said to it.

"Ah, the strange enigma of a vampire has come before me again. What can I do for you?" said the statue.

"What do you know of portals?" asked Erip Mav.

"Why do you want to know about portals?" asked the dragon statue.

"I mean to release the demons," said Erip Mav calmly.

"Oh, you do?" said the statue. It wasn't really a question. "Then, you should know that they will never serve you. Opening portals is quite simple."

"It is?" asked Erip Mav.

"Yes, indeed it is," said the dragon statue.

"Then how do I do it?" inquired Erip Mav.

"I must decide if you are worthy of the secret. Come back later," said the statue.

"Very well," said Erip Mav. Erip Mav decided to contact his dwarven allies to see how they were fairing. He had recently learned that his seeing stone did not function in the library so he left. He did not like leaving the library. It was a beautiful and alluring place. He departed the library and went to his chambers to activate his seeing stone.

"Lord Mav, it is great to see you," said King Blackfoot Irontoe. His eyes were still very glassy. The magic of mind control was still holding. "How can I serve you?" he asked.

"King Blackfoot Irontoe, how are you today?" said Erip Mav.

"I am well," said King Blackfoot Irontoe. "I have news, My Lord."

"What is your news?" asked Erip Mav. He was intrigued. He hoped that it was good news. In this case he needed news.

"The rebel ship is caught in a cloud funnel storm that is common to the coasts of Orcalias," said King Blackfoot Irontoe. "It has taken them down the coast. This would be an excellent time to surround them with our fleet."

"That is excellent. Surround them and crush them," said Erip Mav.

"It shall be done, even as thou hast commanded," said King Blackfoot Irontoe. "We will bring back one hundred and one prisoners for you my Lord."

"See that you do," said Erip Mav. Erip Mav was very excited. He was finally going to capture Maug and his group of rebels.

. . .

They all woke up the next day. They shared their dreams with each other. They were greatly disturbed by their dreams. They made their way up to the main deck. They were surrounded by massive black ships. The ships drew closer and closer. Christian went to the Captain's cabin to get Maug. He knocked on the door. "Maug, you should come out here. The ship is surrounded," said Christain.

"What?!" shouted Maug.

"The ship is—" began Christian. Maug barreled out the door, knocking over Christian in the process. Maug paused and helped Christian to his feet.

"Surrounded, the ship is surrounded. Yes I heard, I was just surprised," said Maug. "Let us confront those who would challenge us." Maug magically enhanced his voice. "Who are you and why are you here?" he asked. There were eight ships around them.

"We are the dwarves of the southern peak of The Shoulders," said a dwarf on the largest ship. "I am Korlak. I am here to escort you back to the dominion of our Lord Erip Mav."

"We will not return with you," said Maug. "Neither will we surrender." Maug yelled a clarion call and his men began to fight. Three dozen of the men and women who were with Maug jumped to the other ships. With their prodigious skill they defeated the dwarves on all but the great ship. "Breath of fire!" shouted Maug. His men ran to the forward of their ship. They poured the oil into the ears of the dragon head and struck their matches at the hole in the top. The fire did not harm the enemy ships.

"You fools!" shouted Korlak. "We are dwarves! We build our ships to withstand fire."

"We have other things that we can do to escape you." Maug shouted back.

"I do not think so," said Korlak.

"How would you know?" asked Maug. Maug was hopeful that they could do something. He did not know, but they had to try. "Get the men and women down to the oars. Double time. I want to ram that ship!" shouted Maug. He hoped that the celestial iron would hold. The beat was set and they were rowing. They began almost flying toward the main enemy ship. With a massive crash they tore through the enemy ship. The other ships began to attack. Taylor the fairy came out on the deck.

"We must leave now," she said. "If we do not leave now we will never escape.

"I know," said Maug. Suddenly there was the sound of ethereal music. Mermaids were surrounding the ships of their enemies. These mermaids were singing to the dwarves with ancient magics. The dwarves soon left.

"Hello, humans," said the Merfolk leader.

"Hello," said Maug. "Thank you for saving us. I am curious, why did you save us? If you expect to be paid there is nothing that we can offer you. We are very poor, and have nothing, save what we brought with us. Allow me to tell you of our mission. We are following a prophecy to the west. We are going to find the rightful prince of Orcalias and restore him to power. If you intend to stop us from achieving our mission, you should know that we will fight you."

"Do you really think that we could defeat merfolk?" Christian whispered to Maug.

"I think if they gave us a reason to, that we would try," said Maug.

"You have nothing to fear from us," the merfolk leader said. "We are here to help guide you on your way. We know the islands that are safe to camp on, and what food is safe to eat. We can help you. Will you allow us to?"

"We would be most grateful for any assistance that you could offer to us." Maug said. The men and women that made up his crew cheered.

"I will stay with you during your voyage," said the merfolk leader. "That is, until we come to the jagged maze. We cannot venture into the jagged maze. We do not know its secrets. In the jagged maze you will be on your own. But we can help guide you there. Come."

"Go to half sail men, switch out on the oars. We need only about twenty people on the oars at present," said Maug. Then he dove off the ship and joined the merfolk leader in the water. They embraced in a hug, as was the custom. "My brother of the sea, how are you?" inquired Maug.

"I am well enough. I will be better when this vampire is vanquished," said the merfolk leader.

"What is your name?" asked Maug. The merfolk leader laughed.

"My name does not translate into your language. You may call me Strong Fins," said Strong Fins, the merfolk leader.

"That is an excellent name," said Maug. "Where would you recommend that we go tonight?" Maug asked.

"There is an island that we can reach by nightfall that I think will be suited to your purposes," said Strong Fins.

"Excellent, I believe that we shall head there," said Maug. They traveled for the rest of the day until they reached the island that the merfolk spoke of. They left the ship anchored and in the watchful care of Strong Fins. Then they went ashore. There were beautiful fruits on this island. Enough to replenish the ship's stores for certain. There was also large game here.

The next day Maug led a hunting party. They caught and killed several dozen geese. Cooked goose was a favorite among the crew on The Purple Dragon. They also caught ten large pigs. Wild boar that were as big as horses. They killed them and salted the meat to be stored in the hold of the ship. They also killed elk and deer that were on this island.

They traveled deep into the jungle of the island the next day. Here they found a beautiful garden. This garden was truly a sight to behold. There were fruits of every color growing everywhere. There were apple trees. There were pear trees. There were peaches, apricots, oranges, lemons, limes, cherries, coconuts, grapefruits, nectarines, mangos, plums and pomegranates. There were also many varieties of vegetables here in this garden.

They were about to help themselves to everything that they could carry when they noticed a house. This house seemed to be grown out of rose bushes. It truly was a beautiful home. An elf came out of the home. "My friends, welcome!" cried the elf.

"Who are you?" Maug asked. Maug was very suspicious. He did not know what to do about this elf.

"I am Lord of this island. You do not need to know my name. My garden is free for the taking. Take as much as you need," said the elf.

"That does not tell us your name. Nor does it tell us why you are here. We are on an urgent mission and we need to know. I am sorry to be so rude and off putting, but we cannot really afford to trust anyone at the moment," said Maug.

"Very well," said the elf. "My name is Alrain. I have lived on this island for thousands of years. I love beautiful islands and plants so I have chosen to remain here. I cultivate this garden in case anyone travels to visit me. I also cultivate it for my own amusement. I love plants, you see. I would not want to live in a world without plants. Please feel free to take anything you wish. It is all perfectly safe to consume. I grow it myself. I sing to it. It is full of nutrients. The animals here are very unique. While I would prefer that you had not killed them, I am aware that humans eat meat. While I have indulged in eating meat on occasion, I prefer the berries and plants. So what say you? Will you take some of my plants to help satisfy your hunger on your journey?"

"Thank you Lord Alrain," said Maug. "We would be happy with any amount of fruits and vegetables that you can spare."

"Excellent," said Alrain. He went into his house and returned a moment later with half a dozen crates. He walked back into his house and returned with half a dozen more. He continued to do this until he had brought them three dozen crates. "Here my friends. These are enchanted crates. So long as you use them to store your food it will not go bad. Take as much as you need."

"Thank you," said Maug. It turned out that they needed a dozen more crates to fulfill their needs. They carried it back to the beach where they had set up their camp. Alrain remained behind at his hut. Everyone was ecstatic about the fruits and vegetables that they had brought back. They were even more impressed with the meat.

They spent a few days on this island planning how best to proceed, and ferrying their crates of food back and forth. They turned half of the meat that they had collected into jerky. The day came that they decided that they should move on. "I am going to miss this place," said Christian.

"I agree," said Red-fang. He had loved hunting here. It was very enjoyable.

"I am going to miss hunting here," said Maug. "But it is time to go." They set sail again. Strong Fins sent a different merfolk to guide them. He had other things to attend to. So they traveled on.

They traveled for many days on the oceans. The merfolk continued to help them on their journey. Eventually they came within sight of another island. "Ho! Land off the port bow!" shouted a voice from the crow's nest. Those who were not busy with other tasks quickly joined their friends on the deck to view the island. Quickly the merfolk guiding them signaled them.

"You must sail past this island. Stopping here would be a grave mistake," said Red Gills.

"Very well, we sail past it," said Maug. They sailed onward. Eventually another island was spotted. The merfolk again warned them not to stop at this island either. So they did not. They sailed onward.

. . .

It had been a few days since the dwarves had contacted him about the Purple Dragon. He sat in the palace waiting for a response. No response came. So he went to the library to search for more answers. When he tried to awaken the dragon statue it would not speak to him. He grew impatient. He began to have self doubts again. Suddenly his seeing stone began to vibrate. A voice emanated from the stone. "Erip Mav!" said the voice. Erip Mav pulled out the stone.

"Hello," he said. Within the stone there was a red skinned figure with four heads and a large body.

"Erip Mav, do you still intend to release us?" asked the voice.

"Yes, I am trying to work toward that self same goal," said Erip Mav.

"Good, do not forget the promises that you have made," said the figure. Then it vanished. Erip Mav was greatly concerned. He was having some serious second thoughts about releasing the demons. He decided to use his seeing stone to contact the dwarves. He said the magic words and the dwarven king appeared.

"M-m-my Lord-d-d Erip Mav," said King Blackfoot Irontoe. "You have contacted me sooner than I expected you too."

"It has been several days and there has been no word from you," said Erip Mav. "Where is the Purple Dragon?"

"M-m-m-my L-l-l-l-ord they escaped," squeaked King Blackfoot Irontoe.

"They what?!" cried Erip Mav. He was so furious that he lost hold of his magic and King Blackfoot Irontoe was released from the mind-spell.

King Blackfoot Irontoe broke the contact. Erip Mav was so angry. He had lost one of his greatest allies through his own carelessness. What was he going to do now?

. . .

Soon the crew of the Purple Dragon began to see great rocky crags springing forth from the water. Strong Fins again appeared. "Ahead lies the entrance to the jagged maze. As I said, we cannot travel there. You must escape the maze unscathed in order to reach the other side of the ocean. Goodbye my friends." With that the merfolk left.

Chapter Fourteen
The Jagged Maze

There was a great feeling of trepidation as they approached the great maze. There were many questioning murmurs from the crew. Many of them believed that they should not continue on their path through the maze. After many long and hard discussions, they realized that they had no choice. They found themselves talking about if they should turn around.

"It is too dangerous," said one woman.

"I agree!" said another man.

"We cannot turn around now!" cried Christian.

"You are correct!" said Maug. "We must go on." They began to argue among themselves so much that finally Taylor interrupted.

"I, for one, think that we must continue. I recommend that we have a good night's sleep, and begin again tomorrow. I think that tomorrow we will have clearer heads and sharper minds," she said.

Everyone agreed that they should do this. So they all returned to their cots or their hammocks and went to sleep. That night they all experienced nightmares about the horror that awaited them if they should fail. The horror would not just affect them; it would affect the entire universe.

So in the morning they decided to depart. They had no idea what they were going to find inside. They entered the maze and began to travel within it. It was not long before they reached their first obstacle. This obstacle came in the form of a great rock wall blocking their path. "How do we get past this?" asked Christian.

"I do not know," said Maug. "I am open to suggestions."

"How about we try to go around it," said Gray-claw.

"Worth a try," said Maug. "Half sail, turn to port eighty degrees then head straight on. We are going to try to go around it." No sooner had they tried to go around it, then it moved to block their path. "Well that didn't work. Any other suggestions?"

There was a woman among them who had experience with magical allusions. She was very brilliant and her father had been one of the foremost scholars in Orcalias. She was chosen to take his place as Head Scholar. The Head Scholar had access to the fastest horses, the keys to the libraries throughout the country, and many things besides. She was devastated that the takeover had stolen this life of learning from her. She was determined to claim it back. So she had joined this expedition. She thought that she would be able to provide insight and help in their attempt to restore the rightful order. Her name was Monica.

"What if we try to go through it," she said.

"What do you mean?" asked Christian. "That wall is solid rock. If we try to go through it we will be crushed."

"I do not think so," said Monica. "First of all our ship is reinforced with celestial iron. So even if we crash headlong into rocks we will survive. Secondly this maze is designed to deny us passage to the lands beyond. We must reach those lands. It seems to me that there would be some illusions. Illusions designed to trap us so that we cannot escape. I do not know what you think, but I think that we should try to sail through it."

"I had forgotten about the celestial iron," said Christian.

"Is celestial iron impenetrable?" said Blue-foot, he was one of Christian's siblings.

"I do not know," said Monica.

"Maug, do you know?" asked Blue-foot.

"I am not entirely sure. I know that we withstood the strange balls that the wretched vampire launched at us. I feel that they would have shredded a regular ship to pieces," said Maug.

"I think that we should put it to a vote," said Blue-foot. "That way everyone has an equal voice.

"I agree," said Christian.

"Very well, let's call everyone up here on deck and down from the crow's nest," said Blue-foot. It took several minutes to gather everyone up on the main deck. Once everyone was assembled Maug spoke.

"Alright, we have a choice. We can either sail at that wall of rock or turn around," said Maug. "All in favor of sailing through that wall of rock say 'aye'" One hundred voices echoed around the ship.

"AYE Sir!" They all said.

"Go to full sail. Full ahead. Get down to those oars. Double time. If it is not an illusion we are going to bash it hard," said Maug. They went to full sail and plowed ahead. Right before they would have collided with the wall of rock it disappeared. "Well, good call Monica. We shall have to listen to you again if we encounter an obstacle." Monica thanked him and bowed.

"It was merely a lucky guess," she said. She was a very humble person. Her father had taught her that her abilities were gifts, and that she should treat them as such. As a result she learned humility.

"Shall we sail on?" asked Maug. Everyone agreed to sail on, so they did. They spent many days on the water. They had to move slowly to navigate this maze. As they did so, it became apparent that they would either escape the maze or remain trapped in here forever. There was no turning back. Eventually they came across another ship.

"Ahead, off the port bow. I see a ship," came Christian's voice from the crow's nest. As they drew closer to the ship they could all see it. It was a ghost ship, or so it appeared.

"Drop the anchor. Prepare the long boats. We are going to explore that ship," said Maug. He asked for volunteers to join him on the other ship. Only Red-fang, Gray-claw, Christian, and Monica wanted to join him. He left Taylor in charge of the ship. He and the four others got into a long boat and made their way over to the ship. On their way over Monica expressed some concerns.

"Maug, I am worried. What if we become trapped on that ship?" she asked.

"What do you mean?" asked Maug.

"Well, what if that ship itself is a trap?" asked Monica.

"I still do not understand," said Maug. Monica was a little exasperated now.

"Maug, what if there is magic over there and we get stuck on that ship?" she said with a hint of anger in her voice.

"Ah, now I understand you," said Maug. "I apologize, this maze is distracting. I do not think that it is a trap. If it is a trap, then I think that we can escape it."

"Very well," said Monica. They spent the rest of the trip in silence. They arrived at the ghost ship and disembarked from their ship onto the ghost ship. When they were on the ghost ship, everything went icy cold.

"I think that you may have been right," said Maug. They were then each seized by an invisible force. A voice spoke to them.

"Why have you entered our domain?" The voice was a powerful whisper, icy cold. It pierced and seemed to freeze their hearts. There was a powerful quality that caused them to feel cold with fear as they listened to that voice. Their bodies grew very cold.

"What do you mean?" said Maug. "Is your domain this ship?"

"This ship and the waters around it are our domain," said the voice. "Why do you disturb usss?" The last word ended with a hiss.

"We are sorry. We didn't mean to disturb you," said Maug. Maug had become very nervous. "We were curious. That is all."

"Why are you the only one who speaks?" said the voice.

"I am their leader. I represent them. I do not speak for them, rather I speak with them," said Maug. "Do you understand?"

"I believe so," said the voice. "We do not tolerate trespassers within our domain. You will now be terminated." A figure holding a sword appeared. The figure was ghostly clear, as was his weapon. As he raised his sword to strike Maug, Maug lifted his staff and deflected the blow.

"Who are you that would stand against us?" said the voice.

"I am Maug. I am mentioned in the third volume of the book of prophecy. I am searching for the Prince of Orcalias," said Maug.

"Enough!" said the voice. "You will all surrender to us." He raised his sword again.

"Wait!" shouted Maug. "I have not finished telling you who we are."

"Very well, proceed," said the voice.

"We are some of the last free people in this land. It will be easier if we can communicate telepathically," said Maug.

"Very well, we will take what we want from you," said the voice. Suddenly Maug was attacked. Many different voices roiled in his mind at one time. They took from him the memories they sought regarding the current predicament of the land. "Are we to understand that you represent the hopes of all free people? That you seek the rightful prince to restore the government? You seek your way through the maze?"

"Yes," said Maug.

"Centuries ago we too sought our way through the maze. We became trapped here. We became ghosts and decided to haunt those who traveled here. We would not allow others to possess what we could not. Now you come, telling us that you are the last hope of free men. Indeed all free creatures," said the voice.

"Yes," said Maug.

"We could grant you safe passage," said the voice.

"We will do anything to gain free passage," said Maug quickly. They had to succeed in their mission. They had to find the prince. "What can we do for you? We will do anything."

"Will you do what we ask of you?" asked the voice.

"Absolutely!" cried Maug. He had become desperate to escape. He was uncertain if they would be able to escape.

"Burn the ship," said the voice.

"I beg your pardon," said Maug.

"Our ship. Our spirits are tied to it. If you burn the ship we will be released," said the voice. "We will finally be able to rest."

"I see," said Maug, pondering.

"Will you burn our ship or not?" said the voice.

"Yes, we will burn your ship," said Maug.

"Then we release you," said the voice. Maug and his companions got into their long boat and began to row back to the Purple Dragon.

Monica asked "Did you know we would make it out safely?"

"No," said Maug. "but I had hope."

"I see. Maybe next time you will listen to me?" asked Monica.

"Yes, next time I will better heed your counsel," said Maug. They spent the rest of the journey in silence. When they arrived back at the Purple Dragon, they lined up the ropes and were raised back to the main deck.

"Maug, my husband," said Taylor the fairy. "What do we have to do?"

"I want everyone up on deck now," said Maug. They complied and within a few minutes they were all on deck. Maug snapped his fingers and produced a flute. He played the ancient funeral lays of his home. Then he ordered his men to line up the dragon's head with the ship ahead of them. His men complied. He called all the men and women aboard to attention. "Pour the oil." He said. Two men, one on each side of the dragon's head poured the oil into its ears. "Light the fire!" shouted Maug. One man struck the fire into the top of the dragon's head. The two men then began to pump the bellows. With a great whooshing sound fire roared forth and consumed the ship in front of them. This was powerful, like dragon fire. The ship was reduced to ash in a matter of seconds. There was a long shrill scream. Then all was quiet.

"Thank you Maug," said a voice. "Now, we can finally rest." Then everything was still, very still. After a moment of silence Maug spoke.

"Well that's that. Now we can move on." He said. The crew was quiet with a reverence for what they had done. They had released tormented souls. This was a very powerful act. They would all remember this for the rest of their lives. They had released those tied here to the worlds beyond. They began their journey again.

The maze was difficult to traverse. They had to travel in many directions, and they constantly had to change directions to avoid the walls of the maze. Then they came to a great open space. There were four channels ahead of them that they could travel down. There was also a small island ahead of them. On the island there were several sphinxes.

"Well, here are some travelers attempting to get through the maze," said the first sphinx.

"Yes, new travelers, hmm who will they choose?" said the second sphinx.

"Or will they choose us all?" said the third sphinx.

"Hello," said Maug. "What is the point of the three of you?"

"Right to the point this one, isn't he?" said the first sphinx. "Very well. We guard the passages ahead. We will each ask you three riddles. Answer all nine riddles correctly..."

"And you will be given the correct passage," continued the third sphinx.

"Answer between eight and six riddles correctly and we will give you a passage that is dangerous but will still lead to your goal," said the second sphinx.

"Answer between five and three riddles correctly and you will have to traverse much danger before reaching the end," said the third sphinx.

"And, answer two or less riddles correctly and the passage you must use will take you back to the beginning of the maze." Finished the first sphinx.

"What's to stop us from choosing our own passage?" asked Maug.

"If you do not go where we tell you we are free to leave the island and attack you," the three of them said in unison.

"Very well," said Maug. "How do the riddles work?"

"We will choose a champion from among you. If he or she answers all three riddles correctly then he or she may continue answering riddles or choose the next champion. Things will continue in this manner until you get a riddle wrong or you prevail through all nine riddles," said the first sphinx.

"Understood," said Maug. "Who do you choose to be your first champion?"

"We want the were-boy Christian," said the three in unison. "Put him in the long boat and send him to the island. This is the way, he will not come to harm."

"Very well," said Maug. "Christian, get in the longboat and go to the island. You have it within you to answer at least three of their riddles. Be not afraid, only believe in yourself." So Christian entered the longboat and rowed to the island.

"Hello young werewolf," said the first sphinx. "My name is Purple-tongue. Are you ready to begin?"

"Yes," said Christian.

"Very well," said Purple-tongue. "Your first riddle is this: You carry it everywhere you go, and it does not get heavy. What is it?" Christian was afraid. He tried to think but his mind had gone suddenly blank. He was going to let his friends down and doom their quest here and now. As he thought he remembered something that his adoptive father had once told him, "Christian, always be proud to carry your name."

"Your name," said Christian.

"Very good," said Purple-tongue. "Your second riddle is: The more there is, the less you see. What am I?"

"Darkness," said Christian. The sphinxes were becoming very frustrated. But there were still seven more riddles.

"Very well," said Purple-tongue. "The final riddle that I will give to you is: A word I know, six letters it contains, remove one letter, and twelve remains. What am I?"

"Dozens," said Christian.

"Very well," said Purple-tongue. She was seething with anger.

"It is my turn to give you riddles," said the second sphinx. "Will you stay or will you choose a new champion?"

"I will stay," said Christian.

"Very good. My name is Tufty," said the second sphinx. "Are you ready for your riddles?"

"Yes," said Christian.

"Very well," said Tufty. "Your first riddle from me is: What has golden hair and stands in the corner?"

"A broom," said Christian.

"Very good," said Tufty. "Your second riddle from me is: What spends all the time on the floor but never gets dirty?"

"Your shadow," said Christian.

"Very well. You have done excellently so far," said Tufty. "Your third riddle from me is: What falls, but never breaks? What breaks, but never falls?"

"Night and day," said Christian.

"Very good," said the third sphinx. "My name is Taron. Do you elect to choose a new champion? Or will you answer the last three riddles."

"I will continue," said Christian. Back on the ship he heard

Maug swear. The riddles would only get more difficult from here. Christian knew that he could handle this.

"Very well. Would you like a break or would you like to proceed with the riddles?" asked Taron.

"I am ready to proceed with my riddles," said Christian.

"Very well," said Taron. "Your first riddle from me is: What comes in a minute, twice in a moment, but never in a thousand years?"

Christian pondered for a moment. Then he said "The letter M."

"Good," said Taron. "Your second riddle from me is: What can you hold in your left hand but not your right?"

"Your right elbow," said Christian.

"Very well," grumbled Taron. "Your third and final riddle from me is: What goes on four legs in the morning, on two legs at noon, and on three legs in the evening? You will never be able to answer this riddle and you will be ours."

"On the contrary. I can answer that riddle," said Christian. "The answer is A Human."

"Arg!" snarled the three sphinxes. They all ran forward and tried to pounce on Christian. They were repelled from him. They could not touch him. When they finally stopped trying to attack him they said. "Very well, you have bested us at the riddles. Take the channel to the far right."

"Thank you," said Christian with a bow. In short order Christian returned to the ship.

"You did well," said Maug. "I was afraid when you did not pass the riddles off to someone else. Forgive me for losing faith in you."

"There is nothing to forgive. I could easily have lost the riddle game. We take the far right channel," said Christian.

"Shall we be off?" asked Maug.

"Yes!" everyone shouted in unison. They departed through the farthest right channel. They continued their way through the maze. They thought that they would have many more days to go before they reached the end of the maze. So they were glad that they had come prepared.

They traveled for many days before coming to a fork in the path. They did not know what way to go. They dropped their anchor and decided to stay a while. They had to ferret out the secret here. The next morning, shimmering clouds formed words in front of the fork.

If onward you would go then the left path you must take. You will face a great decision. You will have to face your fate.

You could take the right path, it would lead you true. Back to the entrance to the maze your journey began anew.

The choice you face is a powerful one. You must not falter, you must not run. If your journey you would make, take the left path when it is late.

If you would turn your back on your quest, take the right path I do not jest. But if you take the path to the gate you must be careful of the brew.

"What do you suppose that means?" Maug asked. It was his wife, Taylor who answered.

"We must take the left path when it is late of course. We shall take the left path tonight," she said. "Then we will have to watch the brew. I am uncertain about this part of the passage. Christian, do you have any input here?"

Christian remained silent. He remained silent for so long that they began to worry about him. Then he spoke, and when he did it was with power and great authority. "My friends let us continue down the left path. I think the passage means that we must be careful when accepting brew from strangers."

"I agree," stated Maug. "Weigh anchors. Go to full sail. Full speed ahead. Down the left path we go." The men obeyed his orders and brought them to full sail. Within minutes they were at the entrance to the left passageway. "Drop the anchor. We will wait here until nightfall."

And so they did. When nightfall came they continued down the left path. Then the world spun. It was as though the floor was the sky and the sky was the floor. "What do we do?" asked Christian.

"I do not know. I have never seen magic like this," said Maug. Then with a pop a man appeared on their ship.

"Hello strangers. What be ye about?" He said.

"Our errand is our own," said Maug.

"Ah, me friends, I meant no offense. I have simply come to offer you this potion. It will flip the world again and make all things right." He said.

"We have no need for your potions," said Christian.

"Wait, he said that the potion would set the world right again," said Gray-claw.

"Yes, so he did," said Red-fang. "We should listen to him."

"We can listen," said Maug. "What exactly do you think is wrong with the world?"

"Can ye not see it?" asked the stranger. "The world is flipped. Everything is not as it should be! My potion will make things right again."

"Does your potion do anything else?" asked Christian.

"Ah, well why ye be asking me that?" said the stranger. "If it will make the world right, what difference does it make?"

"I want to try this potion," said Gray-claw.

"I agree," said Red-fang. The rest of the travelers on the ship were more skeptical.

"Oh, you can trust me, me friends! I will not harm you!" said the stranger. Everyone on the ship began to slowly become more believing in this stranger. Except for Christian and Taylor the fairy.

"Let us use his potion to make the world right," everyone cried.

"Wait a moment," said Taylor. "What if he wants to seduce us into serving him?"

"We don't even know him," said Christian. "He cannot be trusted."

"Christian is right," said Taylor.

"You don't need to know someone to trust them," said Gray-claw.

"No, you don't," said Christian. "But it is much better that way." The whole time that they had been talking Red-fang had been edging closer and closer to the stranger.

"What are you doing, Red-fang?!" cried Christian. For Red-fang was now close enough to touch the stranger, or to pick up the potion.

"We trust him!" shouted Red-fang. At that very moment Red fang reached for the potion. Christian sprang forward and kicked it from the stranger's hand. The potion sailed in a high arch out of the ship and into the water.

"Now look at what you have done!" said the stranger. With a pop he disappeared. Then, with a very unpleasant lurch the world was right again.

"What happened?" asked Red-fang.

"I do not know," said Gray-claw.

"You, Red-claw, very nearly did something stupid because you became enchanted by a strange man. It doesn't matter though. All is well now," said Christian.

"Shall we be off?" asked Maug.

"Yes," said everyone.

"Let's go, full sail. Get everyone down to work the oars in shifts," shouted Maug.

Everyone moved about in a frenzy to carry out his orders. They had been in this maze for several months. They did not know what to do. There were rumours that one could never get out of the maze. They believed in their leader Maug, they also believed in his second mate Christian. The trust that they put in those two was absolute. For if the crew did not trust them, they were dead.

They continued on their journey through the maze. It was very difficult. Sometimes they faced great storms that pushed them back. At other times they became caught in powerful whirlwinds that would spin the ship around, around, around and around. One day they were visited by a powerful being. Suddenly their ship stopped.

"What is going on?" shouted Maug, running out of his cabin.

"We don't know," said Christian. "All of a sudden we just stopped." There was a great rushing sound. They couldn't quite determine where it was coming from. There was a crack of thunder. There was a streak of fire. There was a great torrent of water. There was a great jerk, and then the ship lurched forward. Suddenly they were no longer in the maze.

Their ship was floating in the air in a great council chamber. There were giant men and women seated in fifteen seats in a circle around the ship.

They looked up and saw Zeus sitting on the throne directly in front of them. They knew that this was his name as it was inscribed below his throne in giant letters. His eyes glowed as if with electricity. His hair glowed like the sun. He was obviously the ruler here.

The man to Zeus's right had hair of deep blue and eyes like emerald pools. This man held a trident made of oricalcum, glowing with an inner light. His robes flowed like water. He had an air of depth about him. Inscribed below his throne was the name Poseidon.

The man to Zeus's left had eyes that glowed like embers in a fire, and hair that looked to be alight with flames. He held an orange glowing whip. Inscribed below his throne was the name Hades.

Maug and his crew refocused on Poseidon. They slowly turned to their left. Examining the other beings in the twelve other thrones.

The woman next to Poseidon had the name Demeter inscribed below her throne. Her clothing was made of grain and wheat. She was beautiful yet simplistic. Yet, she was all the more beautiful for her simpleness.

The man next to Demeter was very fit. He had a satchel full of letters slung over one shoulder, and a caduceus in his left hand. The inscription below his throne read Hermes.

The woman next to Hermes held an olive branch in her hand. She looked very wise and serious. The inscription on the front of her throne read Athena.

The man next to Athena wore a helmet with wings covering his cheeks. He held a sword in one hand and a shield in the other. His eyes were alit with the fire of war. The name inscribed below his throne said Ares.

The woman who sat next to Ares looked regal. She commanded a certain beauty. Her face was too stern to be truly attractive. The inscription below her throne read Hera.

The man next to Hera looked quite drunk. He had a pipe and a bunch of grapes in one hand. In his other hand he held a wine glass that kept refilling itself. He kept giggling and burping. The inscription beneath his throne read Dionysus.

The woman sitting next to Dionysus was fit and outfitted in hunting gear. She had a bow and arrows strapped to her back. The inscription below her throne read Artemis.

The man next to Artemis had some reed pipes. But he was also the most peculiar. He looked like a Satyr. After a few moments they in fact realized that is exactly what he was. He had great horns protruding from his head; he also had the shaggy legs of a goat. The inscription beneath his throne read Pan.

The woman next to Pan was an exquisite beauty. She was extraordinarily beautiful. Perfect in every way. And the dress she wore accentuated the curvature of her body. She was beauty personified. She smiled at the strangers and her smile was mesmerizing. She glowed with a white aura. The inscription beneath her throne read Aphrodite.

The man next to Aphrodite was very rugged looking. His face was crisscrossed with scars. He held a human shaped toy in his hand. He also held a hammer. The inscription beneath his throne read Hephaestus.

The woman next to Hephaestus was quite beautiful, though not nearly as beautiful as Aphrodite. The inscription beneath her throne read Persephone.

The thrones of Poseidon, Hades, and Zeus were larger than the rest. Those three were represented by water, fire, and lightning respectively. The giant sitting in the lightning throne spoke, and his voice boomed like thunder, and his eyes flashed like lightning.

"I am Zeus. Welcome, humans from Orcalias, to Olympus on Earth."

"Who are you?" asked Maug.

"That is an excellent question," said Zeus. "This form is an avatar. Because of my technology and my abilities with magic I have been taken to be a benevolent god. Those before you are my brothers and sisters. To my right is my brother Poseidon. To my left is my brother Hades. We have brought you here to help you on your journey. I see that your ship has already been outfitted with Celestial Iron. Excellent; we do not have as much to do. You are currently on your journey to find the true prince of Orcalias, are you not?"

"Yes, we are," said Maug.

"I see that twelve of your numbers are were-wolves. They will be helpful. Do you know why I brought you here?" said Zeus.

"No, I had hoped that you would tell us."

"Very well," said Zeus. "I have brought you here to help you on your journey."

"How so?"

"There are creatures that you will face at the end of the maze. They are known as gorgons. They spawned from a woman known as Medusa. You must be cautious. Her children are the Basilisk. Gorgons and basilisk can kill you with a glance. If you make eye contact, you are turned to stone," said Zeus.

"How are we supposed to fight against that?" asked Maug

"It is simple," said Zeus. "You must learn to see with more than just your eyes. If your eyes remain closed then you are safe from being turned to stone. However you must still fight. I will teach you how to see without your eyes." So Zeus instructed each of them on the skill of remote viewing. It took several hours but at last they mastered it. "You may now depart. We will send you back to the place in the maze where we took you from."

"Why don't you come help us?" said Christian.

"Young were-wolf, we do not get involved in the affairs of your kind. It is not our way. You must defeat this vampire on your own," said Poseidon.

"Even if we did come to help you, it would be unfair. We cannot save you from your own failure to be diligent," said Hades.

"Furthermore, I do not believe that these vampires are as dangerous as you make them out to be. You will not need our help. There is no way that they can open up portals to the netherworld. They do not have access to the Dragon Scale Keys," said Zeus. He continued. "If they were to access the keys that would be a different story. However they would then have to learn how to use the keys. I do not think they are capable of this. We do not meddle in the affairs of the more mortal races."

"You are gods though," said Christian.

"We do not get involved. Goodbye," said Zeus, Poseidon, and Hades together.

There was a flash of light, a pillar of fire, a beam of lightning, and a torrent of water. Then they were back in the maze. Immediately they all shut their eyes and *sensed* their way through the maze.

Then they heard a cackling laughter that chilled their bones. They also heard the sloshing sounds of something slithering through the water. Someone came running up onto the deck.

"Hey everyone," said Smyth. "What's going on?! Why is it so cloudy? AHHH!" With a thunk he fell down on the deck. He had turned to stone.

"Smyth!" cried Anna. Anna and Smyth were betrothed to be married. Sadly it was not to be. Then a voice spoke and they heard the slithering and hissing of thousands of snakes.

"Ah, humansss. You will never get passsssssssed usss," said a voice. "We are the final challenge."

"Who are you to stop us from getting past you?" said Maug.

"We are the guardiansss of the exit," said the voice. "We are the Gorgonsss and the Basssilisssk."

"What are you going to do?" said Christian.

"We are going to kill you all," said the voice. "I am the queen of the Gorgonsss. You will join my garden of statuesss, at the bottom of the sssea!!"

"Couldn't you just let us pass?" asked Maug.

"Why would I?" asked the queen. With a flash she was on the ship. She walked up to Christian, without looking he smote off her head with his sword. There was a great scream from the other creatures.

"We know how to defeat you!" shouted Maug. He shouted something and the clouds parted. "Light the dragon fire!" The men scrambled to light the dragon fire. The monsters around them began to fall as they saw their own reflections and turned to stone.

Soon they were all dead. With great splashes they sank to the bottom of the sea.

Tentatively Maug opened his eyes and looked over the edge of the ship and saw the glint of a stone snake before it sank out of sight. Then a voice spoke. The voice emmanted from the water.

"You have done well. The ability that we taught you to see without seeing will now be taken from you. You will no longer need it," said a voice that sounded like Poseidon. "You may now open your eyes and continue on your journey. You may keep the head of the queen of the gorgons. It will still turn living things to stone."

Everyone opened their eyes and were relieved. They were devastated to lose Smyth. It was a great loss to them, Smyth was short for he was a descendant of the dwarves; he was their master smith. He would be greatly missed. They took the head of the queen of the gorgons, and placed it in a bag. Maybe it would have a use later.

"What do we do about Smyth?" said Maug.

"I say that we take him with us," said Christian. "Maybe the elves can help."

"P-p-please," said Anna. "M-m-m-may w-w-we store h-h-h-him in the h-h-h-hold?"

"Of course Anna," said Maug.

"T-t-t-thank y-y-y-you," said Anna.

"Take her below to the galley and get her a hot beverage. Coffee, or tea, or cocoa or whatever is available. It will calm her heart and mind. She needs it. Get some of our strongest men up here to take Smyth down to the hold," said Maug.

"I-I-I-I'm f-f-f-fine," said Anna. "R-r-r-really I am. I am fine." She managed to stop sobbing and speak with only a slight quiver to her voice.

"Even so, you need some sleep. I will let you have my bed for tonight," said Maug. "Taylor, will you take her to our cabin and make her a sleeping poultice?"

"Of course," said Taylor. "Come with me Anna." The two of them left for the captain's cabin. Anna would not have admitted this but she was very grateful for what they were doing for her. She felt loved and cared about here. Then they heard a voice echoing down from the crow's nest.

"Lo! Behind us! Something is following. Approaching fast," cried Andor. There was a great ripple upon the water moving fast toward the ship. With a great boom it rammed the ship. The ship pitched and several dozen people were thrown overboard. They screamed as they hit the water.

"Drop the anchor!" cried Maug. "Were-wolves, overboard with you. Help them back to the ship!" Blue-foot, Red-fang, Gray-claw, Christian, and the other six were-wolves dove overboard. In short order they rescued the people who had been thrown overboard by the violent rocking of the ship. "Is everyone safe?"

"I believe so!" said Christian.

"Good," said Maug. "Any idea what that was?"

"I do not know," said Christian.

"You killed my friendsss," said a voice. It was a massive Basilisk, not just massive, it was enormous. It was over a mile long. "I wasss on the floor of the ocean. I got ssstuck. You dessstroyed my friendsss. My family is gone because of you. I will kill you all for thisss. You will be dead. I will dessstroy you."

"Go down and get the head Christian!" said Maug. "The rest of you get into the hold." Maug hollered up to Andor "Toss me the seeing glass!" The seeing glass was thrown and Maug caught it. He looked ahead into the distance and saw the exit of the maze. They had to navigate around some crags of rock but they were almost out of the maze. The were-wolves remained on the deck.

"We have a plan," said Blue-foot.

"Speak," said Maug.

"What if we lured the basilisk in front of the ship, and then we—" Maug cut him off.

"I understand Blue-foot. How do we lure it in front of the ship?" said Maug.

"One of us will jump off, of course," said Blue-foot.

"And, who pray tell, is going to do that?" asked Maug.

"Well, Taylor can fly right? We thought she would stand the best chance," said Blue-foot.

"I will not allow it!" said Maug.

"It is not for you to allow, I accept," said Taylor. She had just walked out of the captain's cabin. With that she jumped into the air, and she shrunk to the size of a fly. Her voice magically magnified, she said. "Hello Basilisk. Come catch me!" She flew in front of the ship and hovered there. The were-wolves ran to the dragon head and lit the fire. Just as they began to blow the bellows the Basilisk snapped at Taylor. She zipped out of sight. With a great rushing, and roaring sound the final basilisk was consumed by the dragon fire. It let out a screech, a horrible wrenching sound that caused them all to clamp their hands over their ears. Then it was dead. Taylor landed on the deck, and grew to her regular size. She was covered in a sheen of sweat, but unscathed. "I barely escaped its jaws," she said.

"I am relieved that you escaped," said Maug, as he embraced her.

"What do we do now?" ask Blue-foot.

"We exit this maze!" shouted Maug. There was a great cheer from below. "Raise the anchor, let us be off. Christian take your kin down to the oars and tell the rest of the crew to man them. Then return here and speak with me. We have much to discuss."

"Yes Maug," said Christian. It took several hours, but eventually they made it through the maze.

Chapter Fifteen
Shore Fall

In short order they arrived at a beach. They were so glad to have gotten through the maze that they held many celebrations. They sang and they danced, and got drunk with wine and ale. They spent weeks reveling in their accomplishments. They were so grateful that they had escaped the fearsome creatures within the maze. One day Christian went to speak with Maug. It was early in the morning. Christian found Maug standing in the waves enjoying the feeling of the waves crashing into him.

"We have been here for weeks, Maug. When are we going to depart?" said Christian.

"Well, I think that we should depart now. Let us ask the others what they want," said Maug. Soon everyone was gathered together. "What would you that we should do?" asked Maug.

"What if we split into groups?" asked Blue-foot. "Then those groups can gather the things that we need to continue on our journey."

"An excellent plan," said Maug. "I want a were-wolf to go with each group. Blue-foot, you take nine people and head off to search for berries. Red-fang, you head out and search for vegetables. Gray-claw you head off and search for wild game. You six remaining were-wolves go find what you think that we could use. Christian, you, Taylor, myself, and the seven remaining people will stay here to guard the ship."

"Understood," said Christian. The nine groups departed from the beach in search of the items that were needed.

. . .

When night fall came the groups began to return. First, Blue-foot returned. Maug saw him coming from a ways off and hailed him. "Ho! What have you found?" shouted Maug. It was a few minutes before Blue-foot arrived.

"We have found berries in abundance. See, we have found strawberries, raspberries, rakberries, napberries, strangberries, blueberries, blackberries, yellowberries, and many more," said Blue-foot.

"I am pleased," said Maug. "This should help us greatly."

"Has anyone else returned?" asked Blue-foot.

"No," said Maug, "you are the first."

"Very good," said Blue foot. They waited in silence. In short order six of the remaining groups arrived back at the beach. They brought wood, leaves, and many other things that they thought could be useful. They also found an ancient dwarvish cave filled with all sorts of riches. They brought these back as well. They were now only waiting on Red-fang and Gray-claw. Soon they saw Red-fang approaching.

"Look what we found!" shouted Red-fang. "We have found squash, spaghetti squash, carrots, peas, beets, many varieties of peppers, many varieties of potatoes, lettuce, cabbage, parsnips, and many more types of vegetables. This will last us for quite a while."

"Excellent!" said Maug.

"We are just waiting on Gray-claw?" asked Red-fang.

"Yes," said Maug. Soon Gray-claw arrived. He and his group were much discouraged.

"I am sorry everyone. There was no game to be found. Not for a fifteen mile radius around the beach."

"No matter," said Maug with a smile. "We can find game later. Let us rest for the night, and then on the morrow we shall send forth a large scouting party. Go retrieve Smyth from the hold of the ship and bring him ashore. We will take it in shifts to carry him to the realm of the elves."

"Thank you," said Anna. She had grown much stronger over the last few weeks. Taylor had told her of the afterlife that the fairies believed in. It was beautiful that loved ones could be together forever. Anna took hold of this belief and allowed it to fuel her. It gave her strength, believing that even if the elves could not save Smyth that she would see him again.

"Of course," said Maug, with a bow.

"Let us all get some sleep," said Taylor.

"Agreed," said Maug. "Tomorrow we will send a large scouting party forth." With that they all departed to their tents, and turned in for the night.

Chapter Sixteen
The Scouting Party

They awoke the next morning very refreshed. They deliberated long how they should go out scouting for a trail or a path. They were all gathered together near their camp on the beach discussing their options. The argument became very heated. Maug interrupted, "I think that we should leave most of you behind to guard the ship, because a journey ahead would be most dangerous. Perhaps even more dangerous than staying with the ship. I think that myself, Blue-foot, Red-fang, Gray-claw, Christian, Anna, Taylor, Red-eyes, Serena, Laycee, Jaylin, and Tanner should go forth to look for a path."

"I would be fine with that," said Blue-foot.

"As would I," said Red-fang. Eventually everyone agreed on this course of action. Those staying behind did not want to admit it but they were afraid. Those named by Maug set off to search for a path. They traveled for many hours until it was nightfall.

"Do you really think that it was such a good idea to leave the others behind?" said Christian.

"You could have raised your concerns then," said Maug. "I would have listened."

"I have no doubt that you would have listened. I just cannot help but feel something terrible is going to happen," said Christian.

"They are all hardened and capable warriors; they have spent the better part of the last two decades fighting a vampire rebellion that should not have happened. They are all capable men and women. What have you to worry about, brother?" said Jaylin. She was one of Christian's seven siblings that he had been reunited with at the beginning of his quest.

"I know that Jaylin, I know that. I just have a very uneasy feeling about them that's all. I cannot help but feel something is going to happen," said Christian.

"When did these feelings develop?" inquired Maug.

"Not long after we left," said Christian.

"How about this? We travel for four days searching for what we seek. If we do not find anything then we will come back to check on them before setting off again," said Taylor. Being a fairy she was very wise and helpful with compromising.

"I agree with that plan," said Maug. "What say you, Christian?"

"I supposed that works for me." Christian said. They made camp and went to bed that night. Nothing happened. They had decided to travel south east in the morning. Christian was still very uneasy and he could not sleep. When he came out of his tent he was astonished. Everything around him was glowing.

The trees, the bushes, the flies, the shrubs, the wood, their berries, even the soil itself glowed. Everything glowed. It was a magnificent and beautiful sight. He didn't think that he would be able to sleep so he wandered around for a long time admiring the way things looked. Then he heard a voice. "It is fairy magic." He turned and to his astonishment saw Taylor nearby.

"Fairy magic?" he asked.

"Yes," said Taylor. "The fairies live in this part of the world. Their magic, rather our magic, is not as potent as that of the dragons or the elves. However, we do have it. We affect things in a very real way. Watch," she cupped her hands and blew through them. The radiance of the tree in front of her grew until it was as bright as a sun. She quickly extinguished the glow, and it softened to its original radiance.

"That was brilliant," said Christian.

"Thank you," said Taylor.

"Tell me of your people," said Christian.

"What would you like to know?" said Taylor.

"Why did your people, the fairies, leave? Why did they abandon humans?" said Christian. "And why did you remain behind?" Anger flared suddenly in her eyes for a moment.

"We did not abandon you!" she said.

"I am sorry. I did not mean to offend you," said Christian.

"No matter, I am not actually offended. I am just reminded of old wounds that is all. You wish to know why the elves, the dragons, and my people withdrew to the east?"

"Yes, please," said Christian.

"Very well, I shall tell you. There was a time when my people dwelt among humans freely. But thousands of years ago there was a great war. There was a certain human who was greedy for power. His name was Relaeh. He sought out the vampire you know as Erip Mav to make him strong. Erip Mav turned him into a vampire and he soon became the foremost expert in vampire medicine." Seeing the look of confusion on Christian's face Taylor continued. "Yes, vampires too need medicine. He became the foremost expert in vampire medicine and stole into the castle one night. He murdered Athoriad The Just and Mandie his wife in their bed. This was the start of the great war. With our help Pathorian the Wise, son of Athoriad beat the vampires back. We helped him to bind them with powerful magic and trap them far to the north. I am unsure how Erip Mav and his followers escaped their confinement. We bound them with powerful spells. There were millions of vampires killed, and still millions more turned back to humans. You see, unicorns have the power to make a vampire human again. This also makes him mortal. There were a great many vampires who repented of their desire for power. These were healed of their vampirism, and allowed to live out normal lives. The rest of them fought. Eventually the king of the vampires at the time, a vile creature known only as Lord Vampire, convinced us to banish them to the north, thus allowing them to live in peace. This was a huge mistake as you have seen. After the great war my people determined that we could not trust humans anymore. We left. Soon the dragons and the elves left as well. The elves were far superior to you technologically. They left behind their steam bridges, and a stash of cannons that Erip Mav apparently found. The elves destroyed or took everything else with them. They didn't want you to use the technology to kill each other." Taylor sighed. "And this comes to me. I was banished for trying to smuggle technology back to the humans. My father did not want to banish me but the elves demanded it. The banishment was only supposed to last for one thousand years. Then I could return and all would be forgiven. I had grown comfortable in the land of humans and werewolves. I had grown to be used to my people being gone. So I did not return. They sent scouts to find me but I evaded them all. I did not want to return. I feel a certain trepidation about returning. I am afraid. Speak of these things to no one. Maug knows of them; you may discuss it with him, but no one else. Am I clear?" asked Taylor as she finished.

"Yes," said Christian. He was shaken by the things that he had heard. He did not know what to think.

"Good," said Taylor. She stood up and turned to return to her tent. It was almost dawn. Before she walked out of sight Christian spoke.

"I am sorry," he said. Soon everyone was awake and they broke camp. They weren't traveling in a specific direction, mainly just looking for a trail. Christian caught a moment alone with Maug. "Maug, I..."

"She told you," said Maug, it was not a question. Somehow he knew.

"Yes," said Christian.

"Guard that knowledge well," said Maug.

"Why did she choose to tell me?" said Christian.

"I would guess for the same reason that the guardian dragon allowed you into the vault," said Maug. Christian looked astonished. Maug's deep booming laugh rolled over the hills. "You think I didn't know about the vault? There is a copy of the prophecy hidden somewhere in my tree house. I have no idea how to access it. It is a good thing that you were allowed into the vault."

"Yes, I suppose it was," said Christian.

"Now, let us join the others. I would like to set up camp," said Maug.

"Yes, sir," said Christian. They regrouped with the others who were not far off and they set up camp. They enjoy drinking around the fire and telling stories. Taylor showed them how to clean their hands with the sap from certain trees, then they all turned in for the night.

That night the world was bent. Christian was running along a beach, searching for his friends. They were nowhere to be found. He searched for hours and hours, and traveled many miles but he still could not find them. With a scream he awoke. The others came running.

"Christian, what is it?" asked Maug.

"I had a horrible dream that our companions disappeared from the beach, and that our ship is gone!" cried Christian.

"We must leave quickly!" said Maug. In a few hours they arrived at the beach. Everyone was gone, their ship was gone, all that remained was the statue of Smyth.

Chapter Seventeen
Ship Missing

Erip Mav was frustrated beyond measure. He sat in their chambers pacing. "Come join me, my love," said Taylee. She lay in their bed waiting for Erip Mav to join her. They had just enjoyed a wonderful night feasting on the many blood dishes. She could still taste the blood on her lips, and she savored it.

"I cannot," said Erip Mav. "I am distracted."

"Why my love?" said Taylor. She rose from the bed and wrapped her arms around him.

"Those blasted rebels have escaped!" shouted Erip Mav. He broke from her embrace and stalked to the window. He looked out over the city. He did not know what to do. From behind Taylor approached him once again. She embraced him again. This time he did not break from her grip.

"What else is wrong, my love?" said Taylor.

"The spell that was controlling Blackfoot Irontoe has been broken. I do not have the dwarves with us anymore. With the spell broken his healers will realize that something is wrong. They will heal him from the gold sickness I gave to him," said Erip Mav. "Then they will ally themselves with the werewolves and attack us. Our son will be in danger."

"Oh fear not, my love. All will be well. Come join me in our bed. Kiss me, let us embrace," said Taylor. Erip Mav kissed his wife and they were caught in an intimate embrace. Together they stepped toward the bed.

That night Erip Mav dreamt something strange. *As he held his seeing stone a dark entity touched his mind. This entity showed him how to work the Dragon Scale Keys. At least in part, how to work them.*

The next morning Erip Mav took the dragon scale keys with him to a courtyard outside the palace. He summoned Lightning and Leecher. "Hello, Lord Erip," they said as they arrived. "What are we going to do today?"

"We are going to test the dragon scale keys again," said Erip. "I had a dream last night. I think I know how to make them work."

"What, pray tell, was this dream?" asked Leecher.

"I dreamed that the keys have to interact with something that is the same color as them," said Erip Mav. He snapped his fingers. A tree, a bucket of water, a purple pumpkin, a flaming log, and a yellow ball appeared. "Now, take the yellow key and the ball Lightning. Be sure to electrify the ball. I will take the bucket of water, and the blue key. Leecher you take the flaming log, and the red key. I will count to three. On three I will plunge my key into the water and twist it, Lightning will plunge the yellow key into the electrified ball and twist it, and Leecher will plunge his key into the fire and twist it. As we twist our keys we will imagine the realm of the ancient gods. Do you understand?"

"Yes," they both said in unison.

"Very well. One, two, three." They twisted the keys and thought of the realm of the ancient gods. There was a flash of light.

Then a boom. There was a swirling circle in the sky. It looked like a pool of circular water in the air before them. They stepped through it. Then they were standing in a great chamber. They were blinded for a moment before their sight began to return.

"Who. Are. You?" boomed a voice. They were in a beautiful chamber. Surrounded by fifteen thrones in a circle. They were mesmerized by the beauty of the chamber. The walls were made of oricalcum. There were beautiful statues everywhere. They were so taken in by the beauty of the statues in the chamber that they were distracted. So distracted in fact that they failed to respond to the voice that spoke. They were mesmerized as they began staring at the beings around them sitting on the thrones.

They looked up and saw Zeus sitting on the throne directly in front of them. They knew that this was his name as it was inscribed below his throne in giant letters. His eyes glowed as if with electricity. His hair glowed like the sun. He was obviously the ruler here.

The man to Zeus's right had hair of deep blue and eyes like emerald pools. This man held a trident made of oricalcum, glowing with an inner light. His robes flowed like water. He had an heir of depth about him. Inscribed below his throne was the name Poseidon.

The man to Zeus's left had eyes that glowed like embers in a fire, and hair that looked to be alight with flames. He held an orange glowing whip. Inscribed below his throne was the name Hades.

The vampires refocused on Poseidon. They slowly turned to their left, examining the beings in the twelve other thrones.

The woman next to Poseidon had the name Demeter inscribed below her throne. Her clothing was made of grain and wheat. She was beautiful yet simplistic. Yet, she was all the more beautiful for her simpleness.

The man next to Demeter was very fit. He had a satchel full of letters slung over one shoulder, and a caduceus in his left hand. The inscription below his throne read Hermes.

The woman next to Hermes held an olive branch in her hand. She looked very wise and serious. The inscription on the front of her throne read Athena.

The man next to Athena wore a helmet with wings covering his cheeks. He held a sword in one hand and a shield in the other. His eyes were alit with the fire of war. The name inscribed below his throne said Ares.

The woman who sat next to Ares looked regal. She commanded a certain beauty. Her face was too stern to be truly attractive. The inscription below her throne read Hera.

The man who sat next to Hera looked quite drunk. He had a pipe and a bunch of grapes in one hand. In his other hand he held a wine glass that kept refilling itself. He kept giggling and burping. The inscription beneath his throne read Dionysus.

The woman sitting next to Dionysus was fit and outfitted in hunting gear. She had a bow and arrows strapped to her back. The inscription below her throne read Artemis.

The man next to Artemis had some reed pipes. But he was also the most peculiar. He looked like a Satyr. After a few moments they in fact realized that is exactly what he was. He had great horns protruding from his head, he also had the shaggy legs of a goat. The inscription beneath his throne read Pan.

The woman next to Pan was an exquisite beauty. She was extraordinarily beautiful. Perfect in every way. And the dress she wore accentuated the curvature of her body. She was beauty personified. She smiled at the strangers and her smile was mesmerizing. She glowed with a white aura. The inscription beneath her throne read Aphrodite.

The man next to Aphrodite was very rugged looking. His face was crisscrossed with scars. He held a human shaped toy in his hand. He also held a hammer. The inscription beneath his throne read Hephaestus.

The woman next to Hephaestus was quite beautiful, though not nearly as beautiful as Aphrodite. The inscription beneath her throne read Persephone.

"We are from the land of Orcalias," said Erip Mav.

"How did you get here?" asked a woman. Now that they were facing Zeus again she was seated to their right. They once again saw that she was extraordinarily beautiful. Perfect in every way.

"Who are you?" asked Leecher. He was clearly enthralled with her beauty. So enthralled that he began to drool slightly.

"I am Aphrodite. I am a member of the Council of the Fifteen," she said. She laughed at him as he drooled at her. "Now, how did you get here?"

"We used these," said Lightning. He held one of the dragon scale keys up for them to see.

"How did you get those?" asked Zeus. "They are supposed to be locked away safely in a protected vault."

"The Guardian Dragon told me that I was pure in heart," said Erip Mav. Hera laughed.

"You, vampire, pure in heart?" She asked. "How could a creature so vile be pure in heart?"

"I concur," said Aphrodite.

"I do not know," said Erip Mav. The other gods began arguing in a clamoring. They even left their thrones and began yelling into each other's faces. Soon Zeus was fed up with the arguing. He stood and his voice boomed like thunder through the room.

"Enough!" shouted Zeus.

"Forgive us, brother," the fourteen gods said in unison.

"All is well. You are forgiven," said Zeus. "What are we going to do with these three?"

"I vote that we kill them!" shouted Ares, his voice cracked like cannon fire.

"Ares, you are so predictable. You always shoot first and ask questions later. I suggest we study them," said Athena. Dionysus giggled.

"Why should we study them?" said Dionysus as he took a long pull from his pipe.

"Why indeed," said Pan. "They do not love the land. They are killers and destroyers."

"Wait," said Hephaestus. "We told the other humans that we could not help them. Killing these would be helping them. Let us send them back." Suddenly there was a clamouring. The gods began to argue again. Their arguments grew so loud that the floor began to crack. Thunder boomed as lightning rippled through the room.

"Enough!" shouted Zeus again. "We will send them back."

"Wait!" cried Erip Mav. "We don't even know who you are."

"Hades, Poseidon, assist me. We will send back the one called Leecher and the one called Lightning. Then you will all leave. I want a word in private with the other one," said Zeus.

"Yes, Brother." they replied. There was a flash of light, a torrent of water, a beam of fire, and a strike of lighting. Then Lightning and Leecher vanished. The other gods walked out of the room leaving Zeus and Erip Mav alone.

"A vampire who is pure in heart," said Zeus. "Indeed this is a rare thing. I think that you will have an important role in shaping the world to be. Tell me about yourself."

"I am millions of years old. I am married to Taylee, the granddaughter of the previous king. I have fathered a child with her. She is my beloved and I love her. I do not know why but I feel many doubts about my mission. I have chosen to release the demons."

"You have what?" asked Zeus sharply.

"I have chosen to release the demons," said Erip Mav.

"You are very powerful. As are your wife and child," said Zeus. "Perhaps you should reconsider your mission. It could cause great evil."

"Thank you. I will think on what you have said," replied Erip Mav.

"You must never return here. If you do, I will kill you," said Zeus.

"Understood," said Erip Mav. Zeus summoned Hades and Poseidon back into the room. There was a flash of light, a torrent of water, a beam of fire, and a strike of lighting, and Erip Mav was back outside his own palace.

. . .

Maug and his companions spent hours searching the shore. They were unable to find anything. Smyth was their only clue. He also wasn't much of a clue. "What should we do?" asked Maug.

"I think that we should split up," said Anna.

"Wait," said Blue-foot. "Splitting up is what got us into this mess in the first place."

"Ah, that is true," said Anna.

"Where should we go from here?" asked Christian.

"What if we camp the night and investigate things in the morning?" asked Taylor.

"That is wise counsel," said Maug. They set up a camp and went to sleep. The next morning they awoke to find all of their weapons missing. "Who was on watch?" inquired Maug.

"Blue-foot and I shared the watch, sir," said Christian. "We saw nothing."

"This is true," said Blue-foot. "We did not see anything."

"I think that we should go check out the caves further up the beach," said Tanner. "Maybe we will find what we seek."

"What of Smyth?" asked Anna.

"We could carry him," said Christian, gesturing at the other were-wolves.

"No we cannot," they all said in unison.

"Oh, but we can," said Christian.

"How?" asked Maug.

"We will build a sled. We still have all of our rope and wood. So we shall build a sled and two different were-wolves will transform and carry it every day," said Christian.

"Actually, that could work," said Serena. The other were-wolves agreed. They set to work and built the sled. They set off toward the caves.

"You know," said Maug. "These mountains are so big I doubt that we can climb our way over them."

Red-eyes replied, "I think that there is a tunnel somewhere that will lead us through the mountains."

"Then let us find this tunnel," said Maug.

Chapter Eighteen
Strange Dreams

They made their way up the beach to the caves. The caves were large enough to hold several thousand warriors. They relied on the were-wolves' impeccable sense of time in the caves to know when to stop and rest. When it would have been nightfall on the surface they stopped. They had traveled for a full eighteen hours inside the caves. They did not need their tents here so they laid down to sleep.

Serena had some very strange dreams that night. Strange dreams were nothing new for werewolves like her. If they got too drunk they could transform and forget. Then later they would dream about what they had done. They would also dream about what they had seen.

These dreams were different. *Serena was among people who were worshiping her as an embodiment of nature itself. They called themselves druids. They would bow to her and bring her the food from their tables. They begged her to transform for them so that they could see her magic. When transformed she was very large. She was of an ancient were-wolf bloodline. When transformed she was one and a half times the size of a large brown bear. Simply massive. She traveled among these people for what seemed to be days. Then she encountered a man who seemed to be their leader. "Ah, hello there! My dear, you are a powerful were-wolf. The celtic druids are not used to one as big as you," he said.*

"What is this?" Serena asked.

"Well, put simply this is a vision. It is very real. You are interacting with us; however you are still asleep on the floor of that cave," said the man. He wore purple robes, and carried a white staff. There was a large sword hung at his waist. He had flowing locks of silver hair and a silver beard to match.

"Who are you?" She asked.

"Oh, well I suppose I should introduce myself," said the man with a chuckle. "My name is Merlin. I am a great wizard here."

"Where is here?" She asked.

"Here is the isles of Britannia on Earth my dear," said Merlin.

"Another world? Wait, isn't this the world of the gods?" She asked.

"Right you are!" said Merlin. "Although they are not gods."

"What do you mean?" asked Serena.

"The Council of Fifteen has powerful magic, weapons, and technology. But they are not gods. They are misunderstood travelers," said Merlin.

"What does that mean?" asked Serena.

"You will learn about them later. Someday all truth will be revealed," said Merlin. "You must have many questions."

"I think my questions would be unending if we had the time," said Serena. Merlin chuckled again.

"Probably." He said. "I could probably answer all of your questions. However, now is not the time. You must continue on your journey."

"What do you mean?" said Serena. "We all need rest."

"No!" said Merlin. "You must find your way out of the caves now before it is too late. You will become trapped there if you are not careful! Wake up and GO!"

"But how do I wake up?" asked Serena.

"Open your eyes," said Merlin. Serena opened her eyes and was in the cave again. While she had been dreaming everyone else had also had a strange encounter.

Anna laid down her head. *No sooner had she done so then she encountered a man. "Ah, hello there! My dear, you are grieving. I am sorry about Smyth. The elves, or maybe the dragons should be able to help," he said.*

"What is this? Who are you? How do you know about Smyth?" Anna asked.

"Well, put simply this is a vision. It is very real. You are interacting with me; however you are still asleep on the floor of that cave," said the man. He wore purple robes, and carried a white staff. There was a large sword hung at his waist. He had

flowing locks of silver hair and a silver beard to match. "Oh, well I suppose I should also introduce myself," said the man with a chuckle. "My name is Merlin. I am a great wizard here."

"Where is here?" she asked.

"Here is the isles of Britannia on Earth my dear," said Merlin.

"Another world? Wait, isn't this the world of the gods? They dwell on a place called Olympus?" She asked.

"Right you are!" said Merlin. "Although they are not gods."

"What do you mean?" asked Anna.

"The Council of Fifteen has powerful magic, weapons, and technology. But they are not gods. They are misunderstood travelers. Olympus is their home; it is also their ship," said Merlin.

"Ship? Like The Purple Dragon?" asked Anna.

"No, this ship travels through space," said Merlin.

"What does that mean?" asked Anna.

"You will learn about them later. Someday all truth will be revealed," said Merlin. "You must have many questions."

"I think my questions would be unending if we had the time," said Anna. Merlin chuckled again.

"Probably." He said. "I could probably answer all of your questions. However, now is not the time. You must continue on your journey."

"What do you mean?" said Anna. "We all need rest. I myself have been through quite an ordeal, losing my betrothed like that."

"Yes, I am so sorry about Smyth," said Merlin. "However, you must find your way out of the caves now before it is too late. You will become trapped there if you are not careful! Wake up and GO!"

"But how do I wake up?" asked Anna.

"Open your eyes," said Merlin. Anna opened her eyes and was in the cave again.

Maug encountered a strange man. *"Ah, hello there! My friend. How are you?"* the stranger said.

"What is this?" Maug asked.

"Well, put simply this is a vision. It is very real. You are interacting with us; however you are still asleep on the floor of that cave," said the man. *He wore purple robes, and carried a white staff. There was a large sword hung at his waist. He had flowing locks of silver hair and a silver beard to match.*

"Who are you?" Maug asked.

"Oh, well I suppose I should introduce myself," said the man with a chuckle. *"My name is Merlin. I am a great wizard here."*

"Where is here?" Maug asked.

"Here is the isles of Britannia on Earth, my friend," said Merlin.

"Another world? Wait, Earth. This is where I met with Zeus? The world of the gods then?" he asked.

"Right you are, this is Earth. The gods reside here in a manner of speaking," said Merlin. "Although they are not gods."

"What do you mean?" asked Maug.

"The Council of Fifteen has powerful magic, weapons, and technology. But they are not gods. They are misunderstood travelers," said Merlin.

"Technology, like that which the elves took with them?" asked Maug.

"Yes, although much more advanced than your steam bridges. Someday all truth will be revealed," said Merlin. "You must have many questions."

"I think my questions would be unending if we had the time," said Maug. Merlin chuckled again.

"Probably." Merlin said. "I could probably answer all of your questions. However, now is not the time. You must continue on your journey."

"Wait, there is one thing that confuses me," said Maug.

"What is it?" inquired Merlin.

"How can the Book of Prophecies know my name if those who wrote it cannot truly see the future?"

"Hmm, excellent question. The Book of Prophecy can magically update itself. So, when it became clear that you and Christian were the ones spoken of, the Books would have been updated to reflect that. I could probably answer all of your questions. However, now is not the time. You must continue on your journey."

"What do you mean?" said Maug. "We all need rest."

"No!" said Merlin. "You must find your way out of the caves now before it is too late. You will become trapped there if you are not careful! Wake up and GO!"

"But how do I wake up?" asked Maug.

"Open your eyes," said Merlin. Maug opened his eyes and was in the cave again. While he had been dreaming everyone else had also had a strange encounter.

Taylor, Blue-foot, Red-fang, and Gray-claw all had similar dreams to Maug, Anna, and Serena. They all dreamed about

Merlin. The others were not so fortunate. Their dreams were frightful.

Christian had a fitful dream of being drowned in molten lead for the sport of some blood mad dwarves. As the lead was poured over him he screamed. Then he awoke.

Jaylin dreamed that she was stuck in her wolf form and that she was being hunted for her beautiful fur. She could not turn back to human form. Then she was caught in their trap. She opened her eyes and found herself back in the cave.

Red-eyes was running along the beach, chasing something. He did not know what he was chasing. Suddenly it turned around and attacked him. There was a ferocious fight. He triumphed, however his wounds were great. He lay bleeding out on the sand. Soon he awoke. He was back in the cave with the others.

Laycee was running along the deck of The Purple Dragon when suddenly it pitched beneath her. She fell overboard. There were man-eating fish in this part of the sea. They began to nibble on her. Suddenly Laycee opened her eyes. She was in the cave. Everyone else was awake except Tanner.

Tanner lay on the ground thrashing and screaming. They shook him and yelled his name. But nothing could wake him. Finally, Taylor walked forward. She kissed his brow. He awoke with a start. He absolutely refused to speak of his dreams to anyone. He was never quite the same after that.

"Are we going to move on?" asked Maug.

"I think that we should," said Tanner. "We have not come this far to fail. And those dreams were necessary for us to know that we should move on."

"I agree," said Christian. "We should be off." They continued through the cave. Soon they began to smell pine. Within minutes they were surrounded by trees. They traveled for several miles. The trees were so thick that for a while they thought that they were still inside the cave.

Soon they emerged into a clearing. Then they heard voices speaking in a strange language. Finally a being appeared.

Chapter Nineteen
The Fairies

The being had very long pointed ears. He was shirtless and very muscular. He stood six feet tall. He had a dazzling smile. His eyes were bright green. His shoulder length hair was deep purple. His whole body seemed to glow with magic. There was a bluish hue to his skin. He smelled of roses, and fresh crisp sea air, and something else that they couldn't place. He began to speak and his voice was powerful. He spoke with a lilting cadence to his voice that made him difficult to understand. At least until you got used to it. "My, my, we have not had humans visit here in quite some time. By the look of that companion you have had an encounter with a gorgon, or a basilisk recently. My name is Naran. Who are you?" He said.

"I am Maug. These are my companions. Taylor, who is my wife, Blue-foot, Red-fang, Gray-claw, Christian, Anna, Red-eyes, Serena, Laycee, Jaylin, and Tanner. Smyth is the statue," said Maug. At that moment Taylor stepped forward. She shrunk to her insect size and then back to normal. She also allowed her wings and her fairy ears to be seen.

"Wait," said Naran. "You are *that* Taylor?"

"Yes," said Taylor.

"Hmm, the queen will want to see you," said Naran.

"I know," said Taylor. Naran spoke to some unseen people. Eight fairies appeared to help them carry the statue of Smyth.

"Come, we must depart quickly to speak with the queen," said Naran.

So they left the clearing and headed deeper into the forest. The forest was so thick that it lent a green tinge to everything that they looked at. The smell of flowers, and berries, and the aroma of soil assailed them from all sides.

As they traveled, fairies flitted past them. The fairies came in all shapes, sizes and colors. Some were thin, some were fat. Some were tall, some were short. Some were dark, and some were fair. They continued on their journey for many long minutes. Soon they came to a great palace, grown out of rocks and trees and extending up into the clouds.

"If the rest of you will wait here, I must take Taylor up to see the queen. We will summon you when we are ready," said Jaran.

. . .

Jaran escorted Taylor up to the audience chamber of the queen. The guards barred the way. "Who goes there?" they inquired. Taylor once again allowed her wings and ears to show. The guards gasped and bowed. "My lady," they said in unison. Taylor bade them to stand and they did so. Jaran retreated to entertain their guests, and Taylor opened the doors and entered the throne room.

"SISTER!" exclaimed a voice. A stunning fairy sat on a beautiful throne before Taylor. She jumped up, ran forward and embraced Taylor. They hugged for several minutes.

"Mary, how are you?" inquired Taylor.

"Better now that I have seen you, my sister," said Mary. "Tell me, why have you returned?" In short order Taylor explained about Erip Mav and how he planned to release the demons from the nether-world. She explained about the prophecy. How they were searching for Carlos. Mary gasped. "That is why there is such darkness in our world. Tell me more about you. I sense that you have been intimate with a human."

"You can tell?" asked Taylor.

"Yes, I can," said Mary.

"Don't worry, I kept my vow. We are married. I'm sorry you could not be there," said Taylor.

"That is fine," said Mary. "We haven't got any time to lose. We must take you to the elves. They can help your companion Smyth. The elves will then take you to the dragons. Then, maybe you can be introduced to the prince. I make no promises though. He is heavily guarded. He does not trust very many people. He lives alone with his companion, Amethysta."

"Thank you," said Taylor. "What of my companions?"

"As I have said, there is nothing that we can do for Smyth," said Mary. "However, we can give your companions a comfortable place to sleep for as long as you would like to stay. I will also hold a feast to celebrate the wedding of you and this Maug. I would speak with him. Return to your companions and send me Maug."

"Why do you wish to speak with Maug?" said Taylor.

"I want to know if I can trust him," said Mary. "As you know, as the queen of the fairies I can grant immortality to humans."

"You would do this for him? For us?"

"Yes, my sister. I love you," said Mary. "I would do this for you. Return to your companions and send Maug up. He must come alone."

"Yes my sister," said Taylor. She left the audience chamber, walking through the palace on the way back to her companions.

As she walked through the palace she was taken back to memories of her childhood. The times that she spent playing with her friends and siblings in the palace. This was before the Jagged Maze had been constructed. This was before the dragons, the fairies, and the elves left the humans alone to themselves. Taylor had chosen to fight in the great battle of Orcalias, and this is what led to her remaining in Orcalias. She was caught up in many old memories. So caught up in old memories that she did not realize where she was, when she came to herself she was outside again. Then she reached her companions.

. . .

They were still being attended to by Jaran. Taylor was again overwhelmed by the smell of roses, and fresh crisp sea air, once again there was something that she didn't quite recognize. She tapped Maug and they withdrew somewhat from the others. "My sister, Mary, wishes to speak with you," said Taylor.

"Why?" asked Maug.

"Well, she wishes to know if you will be a good companion for me. She also has something to offer you," said Taylor.

"What does she have to offer me?" inquired Maug.

"You must ask her this yourself," said Taylor.

"Very well. Let's go," said Maug.

"You don't understand. She wishes to see you alone," said Taylor.

"Again, I ask why," said Maug.

"Will you please do this for me?" asked Taylor.

"Yes, of course, my love," said Maug. Taylor gave Maug directions through the palace to the audience chamber where the queen would see him. So Maug left everyone else and went up to see the queen.

. . .

The guards blocked his way. "Who goes there?" They asked.

"It is I, Maug. Husband of Taylor," said Maug.

"Send him in," said a muffled voice from inside the chamber. The guards opened the doors and bade him enter the chamber. He entered, and the doors boomed shut with a powerful finality.

Immediately Maug was assaulted by intoxicating smells. He smelled berries, and plants. The earthy aroma of soil. He also smelled his mother's home cooked stew and the familiar smell of burning wood.

Then he saw her, she sat on her throne. She was regal. She looked much like her sister Taylor. To him Taylor was the more beautiful of the two. This woman had hair of a vibrant, almost glowing blue. It hung to her waist. She held a sword in her hand. She snapped her fingers and a sword appeared in his hand.

"Have at you Maug!" she shouted. She vanished and appeared behind him. They began to duel. She fought ferociously. She swung and struck, blow by blow she began to wear down his defenses. They dueled for nearly an hour. Finally he stopped fighting back, and she stopped mid stroke.

"Why are we fighting?" asked Maug.

"I had to know if you had the skills to defend my sister. I am satisfied that you do. Now, one thing remains. Do you wish to be immortal?" She asked.

"Wait, I don't even know your name," said Maug.

"My name is Mary," she said. "Now, I ask you again. Do you wish to be immortal?"

"Who are you to offer me such a gift?" said Maug.

"Well, I am the queen of the fairies. And while it is true that magic users such as yourself can marry fairies, I do not want my sister's heart to be broken as she watches you die of old age. So I offer you this opportunity," said Mary.

"I accept," said Maug.

"Very well, step forward," said Mary. Maug stepped forward and Mary spoke four words. "Maug, vincortalia nomorteo gaiea." Mary then sagged for a moment. Maug was lifted up in a pillar of light, he screamed as every cell in his body transformed. "There, now you are immortal. Also, I thank you."

"What for?" asked Maug.

"For waiting until marriage to have relations with my sister. You see, fairies make a vow that they will wait until marriage to have relations. However, if they break this vow they lose their immortality, permanently. So again I thank you." Mary snapped her fingers, and a white haired fairy appeared. "Please go fetch my sister and her companions and bring them here. I wish to have a glorious feast with them."

They had a feast that was truly glorious. There were dishes of every kind, mostly having to do with fruits and vegetables. There was no meat to be had here. The feast lasted for two days. Then they slept. The next day they awoke and discussed what they were going to do next. "I think that we should depart forthwith," said Maug.

"I agree," said Christian.

"Could we not stay a few more days?" begged Blue-foot. He had become quite enthralled with some of the fairies.

"Blue-foot, you are getting distracted," said Red-eyes.

"Yes, and for good reason," said Blue-foot. "These fairies are all very attractive."

"I think that we cannot afford for you to get distracted any longer," said Maug. "I say that we depart today."

"Hmm, very well. Fine," spat Blue-foot. "We can leave today."

"Let us go speak with Queen Mary before we depart," said Taylor "She can probably provide us with a guide, and maybe even some fairies to help us carry Smyth."

"Agreed," said everyone else. So they walked through the palace to the audience chamber of the queen. The guards announced them and let them in.

"What can I do for you?" asked Mary.

"Sister," said Taylor with a bow. "We were hoping to have some help. We need some fairies to help us carry Smyth. And furthermore we will need a guide. Can you provide these for us?"

"Of course, sister," said Mary. She snapped her fingers and Naran appeared. "Naran, please guide my sister and her friends to the realm of the elves. Also, find six of your strongest friends to carry the statue of their companion."

"Yes milady." Naran said with a bow.

"Is there anything else that I can do for you?" said Mary.

"Could you give us advice on how to conduct ourselves with the elves?" said Maug. "Anything that we can do to gain their trust would be helpful."

"Be cautious of the elves. They often talk in circles or even riddles. If an elf asks you a question, be cautious how you answer," said Mary.

"Do you have any other advice for us?" asked Maug.

"No. Go, and good luck," said Mary.

"Thank you sister," Taylor said with a bow.

"Yes," said Maug. "Thank you." And with that they departed.

Chapter Twenty
The Elves

Naran escorted them through the forest to an open plan that was several leagues across. Maug asked, "Do the elves live underground?"

Naran chuckled. "No, silly human. See those mountains in the distance?"

"Yes, I do," said Maug.

"The elves live there." Naran said.

"That seems very far away," said Christian.

"Not really," said Blue-foot. "Are they?"

"They are further away than they look," said Naran. "It will take several days to get there."

"Several days of traveling with you?" said Red-eyes. They all stared at him in horror. Naran only laughed.

"I admit that travelling with you too is strange, werewolf," said Naran. "But yes, you are stuck with me for several more days."

"Very well," said Red-eyes.

They traveled on. They spent their nights keeping watch. For as Naran said, "We may live here but the forest still holds many dangers." One morning they woke up, and they knew that they were not alone. Maug drew his staff.

"Who goes there?" He shouted. Then he felt a prick on the back of his neck and lost consciousness. His companions likewise lost consciousness, including Naran, and the six fairies carrying Smyth. When they awoke they were in a dungeon.

"You didn't tell us that we would be locked up!" said Blue-foot.

"I did not know," said Naran. They had an elder fairy with them named R'Yial traveling with them. Naran turned to R'Yial and asked "Do you know what is going on?"

"Well, it is well known that the elves do not trust werewolves. As a fair number of our company are werewolves I would imagine that is why they locked us up. One would have thought that they would have at least talked to us first. Of this I am uncertain," said R'Yial.

"I knew that it was a mistake to come with you and help these beasts," said another fairy.

"Peace, T'Rical," said Naran. "We are friends to all."

"I do not trust werewolves, or humans!" shouted T'Rical.

"What about me?" said Taylor. "I am of your own kin. In fact I am the sister of your queen."

"You think you are trustworthy?" Spat T'Rical. "You betrayed us and stayed with the filthy humans. You even smell like them now."

"Hold your tongue T'Rical!" Yelled Naran.

"It doesn't matter, I am not offended," said Taylor. "He has a right to feel as he does. I know many of you feel this way, however I know that you would never voice these feelings. It is refreshing to have someone brave enough to speak their mind." Maug was seething, he was appalled that the fairy dared speak to his wife in this manner. However because his wife was not offended he would try to control himself. Maug had always had a short fuse when people insulted those that he loved.

"We need to find a way out of this prison," said Blue-foot.

"I concur," said B'Lacti.

"As do the rest of us I think," said Naran. They all heard footsteps. They went deathly silent. An elf with skin the color of ebony walked toward them. He smelled of cedar wood, campfire, and also a little of rum. He spoke with a lilting accent similar to the fairies.

"Who are you?" said the elf.

"Why should we tell you?" spat Red-eyes.

"Well, for one you are in my prison," said the elf. "I do not know if I can trust you. You are strangers traveling on the fringes of our domain. We were well within our rights to capture you. We can also hold you prisoner as long as we wish. If you will not tell me who you are, my brother Jovani wants to see her." He pointed at Taylor.

"She is not going anywhere alone," said Maug.

"Fear not my husband," said Taylor. "I can take care of myself." Maug opened his mouth to protest, but Taylor held up a hand forestalling him. The elf opened her cell and took her with him.

. . .

They exited the dungeon. The dungeon was a tightly clumped group of trees grown together. They walked for several minutes until they came to a great cabin that was grown from living trees. There was a sign that read "Rainhard Hall Home of King Jovani." They walked through the front doors.

They were standing in a great chamber. Trees stood in the place of pillars. The whole place thrummed with magic. It smelled of pine, blue spruce, and the fruity smell of wine. The very air here seemed to shimmer. They began to walk down the hall. Taylor became aware that they were walking toward a throne. An elf sat on the throne. One of his ears had been cut off, and he had long claws on each finger in place of finger nails. He stood and walked toward them. Suddenly Taylor recognized him.

"Jovani!" She exclaimed. Jovani laughed with delight.

"Yes my friend, I am alive," said Jovani. They embraced. Suddenly shocked Jovani stepped back. "You have married a human?"

"Yes," said Taylor.

"Now, that is unexpected," said Jovani. "Tell me why you and your companions have trespassed here."

"I remember a time when you were not so paranoid about visitors," said Taylor.

"Yes, that was when we thought that the vampires were gone for good," said Jovani. "Now we must be careful who comes here. I do not know who I can trust. Now, tell me of your companions."

"There is myself; you know of me. The other fairies are with us only to guide us, and to carry the statue. The statue is a fallen comrade. He looked into the eyes of a gorgon while we were in the maze. Then there is Maug, my husband. Blue-foot, Red-fang, Gray-claw, Christian, Red-eyes, Serena, and Jaylin who are werewolves. Then there is Anna, Laycee, and Tanner, who are humans."

"Fair enough," said Jovani. "I must know why you have come here."

"We search for the prince. The rightful prince of Orcalias," said Taylor.

"What makes you think that you will find him here?" said Jovani.

"Well, for one thing we know that some men at the docks were the last to see him. There was also a boy named Joshua," said Taylor. "Furthermore, we have the third volume of the book of prophecy."

"Very well," said Jovani. "Yes, the boy is here. He was trained by our most skilled warriors and artisans. He can do incredible things. However, he has dwelt with the dragons for the last several years."

"That is curious," said Taylor.

"Oh, not really. I suggested that the boy should fight the vampires who drove him into hiding. He did not like that idea at all. So he left his quarters here and dwells with the dragons now," said Jovani.

"We must see him," said Taylor.

"What makes you think that you can persuade him?" inquired Jovani.

"Well, for one thing I have information about his mother. For another, we did not travel all this way for nothing," said Taylor.

"You never cease to amaze me," said Jovani.

"Thank you," said Taylor. "Is there anything that you can do for Smyth?"

"As a matter of fact, yes, I believe that I know someone who can restore him," said Jovani.

"Oh thank you," said Taylor. "His betrothed will be so happy."

"I must warn you though," said Jovani.

"Yes?" asked Taylor.

"The boy is not to be trifled with. Tread cautiously," said Jovani.

"Thank you. We will," said Taylor.

"Good, now that we have settled that." He nodded at the other elf. "Giovani, go fetch her companions. We now know that Taylor has not fallen, and that they are true allies. They will dine with us tonight, sleep here in the hall, and depart in the morning."

"Yes, brother," said Giovani. Giovani departed and returned within a few minutes with her companions. They also brought the statue of Smyth. When they were all in the hall Jovani pulled a rock out of his robes. He spoke into it.

"Hello my friend, are you there?" said Jovani. All of those present save the elves were astonished. They thought that Jovani was quite mad. They were even more astonished when a voice answered him.

"Yes, my friend Jovani. I am here. How can I render assistance to you?" said the voice.

"I have a petrified human here. Do you think that you could cure him?" said Jovani.

"It would be my honor," said the voice.

"I would be forever in your debt," said Jovani.

"No, there is no debt. This is what I do. I serve the universe," said the voice. There was a very loud bang. There stood a unicorn. The unicorn shimmered for a moment, and then stood in human form before them. He held in his hand a horn. He walked forward, and pressed the horn to Smyth's forehead, while at the same time briefly kissing him on the lips. Smyth seemed to melt as he slowly turned back to normal. He gasped for breath. The unicorn removed the horn from Smyth's forehead.

"T-t-t-thank you," said Smyth. "I am forever in your debt." The unicorn embraced Smyth. And Smyth began to weep.

"There is no debt here. Be thou whole, and be more careful," said the unicorn. He shimmered again and returned to his animal shape. Then with a very loud bang he departed.

"Now that everyone is whole again let us feast!" cried Jovani. He clapped his hands. Tables appeared laden with all sorts of dishes. Everything that you could imagine was here. All of your favorite things and many more. They began to eat, drink, and have fun. There was much going on. The party lasted well into the night. Then they retired to bed.

The next morning the awoke, and thanked the elves for their hospitality. The fairies departed back to their own lands.

"Be cautious around the dragons," said Jovani. "They are powerful." And with that enigmatic advice they departed.

Chapter Twenty One
The Dragons, and the Prince

They only traveled for a few days before they were outside the realm of the elves. Then the road came to an abrupt end. To their left was a great jungle, to their right was a desert. Far, far, far off in the distance were mountains. They were not sure where to go. "Where should we go?" asked Christian.

"I feel good about going into the forest," said Blue-foot.

"Of course you do," said Christian. "You just want to meet a she-wolf."

"You're not wrong," said Blue-foot with a chuckle.

"We really need to decide where to go," said Smyth. He had recovered quickly from his ordeal and was now eager to continue on their journey. The blessing of the unicorn had been powerful indeed. He was now stronger and more fit than he had been before.

"What if we split—" began Red-eyes but Serena cut him off.

"You know what happens when we split up," she said.

"Yes." nodded Maug. "Bad things tend to happen when we are split up. What if we follow the border of the jungle and the desert until we reach the mountains?" After a few more minutes of discussion they agreed that this was the path that they would take.

They traveled this path for several days. Then they were confronted with a great brown dragon. It came diving out of the sky and transformed before them into a wizened old man.

"Who are you?" asked the man. Taylor stepped forward and spoke.

"We seek the prince of Orcalias. We need his help." she said.

"You are a strange group." croaked the man. "Werewolves, a wizard, a fairy, and men."

"Can you help us find the prince?" asked Maug.

"I must know something first." said the man. Then he invaded each of their minds. His touch was gentle. His touch was light. "I merely had to verify your identities."

"We understand," said the group. Then the old man breathed long upon Maug.

"This will identify you to the dragon counsel as a friend of the dragons. If you travel this same path toward the mountains you will eventually encounter the prince. Good luck."

For several more days they continued on their journey. Eventually they were attacked by a pack of manticores. They tried to flee from the manticores but they were soon surrounded. The leader of the manticores spoke to them. "Humans, ah we have not feasted on humans for quite some time," she said.

"What makes you think that you will be able to feast on us?" asked Maug.

"Because you are weak. And we want to," she said. "Devour them!" Then, far above them in the sky there was a glint of purple. A massive purple dragon came diving out of the sky towards them. A young man with silver hair leapt from its back. He drew forth a purple sword, landing in front of the travelers. He held a very unique shield. It looked like the dragon footprints that they had seen. He faced the manticores, and spoke some words in a harsh tongue. The leader of the manticores responded. They spoke for a few moments. Then the manticores retreated. The young man walked toward Maug. Maug was acutely aware that he still had his sword drawn.

"How can I help you?" He asked. The young man seemed wary of the strangers. He had a strange bearing. Not quite the mannerisms of a human.

"Who are you?" asked Maug.

"I am Carlos," he said. "The Prince of Orcalias."

The End

Made in the USA
Columbia, SC
23 July 2021

42264232R00207